Sylvia Liu

MANATEE'S BEST FRIEND

Sylvia Liu

Scholastic Inc.

ISBN 978-1-338-66226-9

10 9 8 7 6 5 4 3 2 1 21 22 23 24 25

Printed in the U.S.A. 40

First printing 2021

Book design by Stephanie Yang

To my family,

David, Sammi, and Sarah

1

The bus ba-bumps over the root-crumbled corner of our street. One more minute and I can escape the other kids chatting and shouting and me trying to be invisible and wondering why I'm not like everyone else. For them, the chance to hang out with friends is one of the best parts of the day, but for me, it's the worst. I never have anyone to talk to, not that I'm brave enough to talk anyway.

At the sight of my house, my body relaxes for the first time since school let out. I'm only moments away from my favorite place in the world, the river by our backyard.

As I hop off the bus, the warm breeze hits me with the sweet scent of yellow jessamines. I take in a deep breath, but my heart revs up when I remember—Missy!

A green anole darts out of my way as I run up the grassy

driveway, drop my backpack by the stairs to our house on stilts, and dash out to the back. I weave past the moss-draped old oaks and head to the river.

Missy's been gone for almost three weeks. Every day after school I come to the water, hoping this will be the day she shows up again.

Missy is a manatee—the gentlest creature, with her round body and stubby snout, always so sweet and trusting. If you didn't know better, you'd think she was just like every other manatee in Florida, but she always comes to eat the eelgrass by our dock, so we've become best friends. Missy is the only one I can talk to about everything—how weird and alone I feel and how I'm constantly terrified of being embarrassed in front of everyone. I never freeze up or have the blood rush to my face or get that sweaty feeling in my palms with her. She doesn't push me to speak up like Mom and Dad do. She's more like Grandma with her Zen-like calm. I'm hopeless at making friends with kids my age, but if I'm only going to have one friend in the whole world, Missy is a pretty good choice.

It's late February, so most manatees are still hanging out in the warm springs upriver, but Missy's been coming by our dock most of the winter. I used to feed her cabbage heads until I found out it isn't a good idea to feed wild manatees. She still visits me anyway. I'm pretty sure that means she loves me like I love her.

I hurry to the end of our dock. An egret startles away like a pale ghost. I'm on the lookout for the white Y-shaped scar on Missy's back, my eyes almost hurting from the strain. It's awful how manatees are recognized by the scars they get from being hit by boats. This is a terrible fact I happen to know because I'll be a manatee scientist one day.

Peering out over the water, I pull out my phone and turn on the video. "Becca Wong Walker, world-famous marine biologist, reporting: It's day twenty of Missy Watch and still no sighting of her." It's for my private online channel where I record my manatee observations, and since I'm the only one who sees it, I don't clam up like I do in front of my class. Normally, this is fun, but now my stomach clenches. Where could she be? I have to keep it together even though my mind is clogged with worry. I say the first thing that pops into my mind. "Manatees can get hit by boats because they're too slow to avoid them. Lately, a lot more boats pass by because new houses are going up along the shore." I scan the water for ripples. "I really hope Missy's okay."

I stop recording and lower my phone. What am I thinking? I'll never have the courage to have my own wildlife show. That would involve talking to actual people, and the thought of that makes my heart speed up and my palms grow clammy.

I sigh. Mom is probably wondering where I am. I should pop back to the house to let her know I'm home. At least there's a bologna sandwich in my near future. Dad gets on my case for eating the same thing every day, but I'm not about to apologize for loving squidgy bread with thin, salty bologna. When I find something I like, I stick with it. Dad also says loyalty is one of the best traits a person can have. I'm very loyal to bologna sandwiches.

A final glance at the water—and I see them.

In the middle of the river, telltale circles ripple one after another across the surface of the water—the sign of a manatee swimming, also known as manatee footprints. I turn the video back on to capture its arrival. "Here comes a manatee," I say. "It's too far away to see any identifying marks."

VVVVRRROOOOM.

A motorboat rounds the bend and zooms straight at the ripples. My throat goes dry, and my body stiffens. I want to scream, *Slow down! You're about to hit one of the best creatures on earth!* But no words come out—they're stuck somewhere between my ribs and stomach. The one and only time I tried to yell at a boat to slow down was a couple of months ago, and when I did, grown men laughed at me. Even thinking about it makes me want to shrivel up and disappear.

The boat continues on, motoring way too fast. I pace back and forth in little zigzags on my dock. My heart pounds. What if it's Missy? *Please don't hit her.*

The ripples have disappeared. The boat zooms away.

My video is still going, so I say, "I hope that manatee's okay."

Finally, the ripples reappear, farther away, on the other side of the river.

I let out a shaky breath. "That was too close. I can't believe those tourists, who just don't care. Or maybe they're locals, who aren't much better." I turn off the video. If I had superpowers, I would've flown off the dock, sped across the water, and punched out the motor. But I don't have superpowers.

I don't even have normal kid abilities, like being able to warn strangers about to hit a manatee.

A few moments pass. I stand up and—

Another set of circles ripple across the water, blooping their way toward me. My heart speeds up again, rat-a-tat-tatting.

Could it be Missy? If Missy were back, I'd have a friend again, instead of always being lonely. I really miss her.

I wish I had my polarized sunglasses. With them on, I could see the manatee's pear-like shape much more easily. I pay special attention for a manatee's nose poking out as it breathes. A large rotund shape slowly swims over.

With a Y-shaped scar on its back.

It's her!

It's Missy.

I slump with relief. She's back, and she's okay.

And next to her is a small shape, like an oval beach ball—a mini Missy! I don't want to scare them away so I clamp a hand over my mouth and squelch the urge to run up and down the dock squealing at the top of my lungs. My grin is so wide my face hurts.

It's a baby manatee.

Oh. Oh. I fumble with my phone and center Missy and her calf in the frame. Missy nibbles at the seagrass, and her baby sticks close by, swimming like a pro. The baby has a small wrinkly face, and its flippers are comically large compared with its body. What a champ, already so self-sufficient.

I narrate in a quiet voice, "Missy's back, and she had a baby! I've never seen a more adorable sight in my twelve years of living on this planet. Look at that cute little bundle of a manatee." I search my memory for more manatee facts.

"Did you know manatees are a threatened species? They only have babies every two to five years. After it's born, a baby manatee sticks with its mama for one or two years. Oh. Oh!" The excited hitch in my voice isn't up to professional standards, but I can't help it. "This little manatee calf will be my friend for at least a whole year!"

Turning off the video and crouching down, I watch Missy's baby swim so earnestly, flapping its stubby flippers to keep up with its mom. "I've missed you so much and was so worried," I tell Missy. "I thought you might've been hit by a boat, but I bet you found a safe place to have your baby. That was really smart of you."

Missy bobs up and down, like she's listening, so I continue. "Let me catch you up on what you missed. School is as awful as usual. I thought middle school might get better now that it's early in the spring semester, and at least I'd have someone to eat lunch with, but no, not at all. I'm still the weird, quiet kid no one speaks to. I feel so invisible."

Missy chomps on the eelgrass.

"Yes, you're right, Missy. I do want to make friends, but it's hard if I can't even say hi to anyone." I sit and dangle my feet in the water. Mom and Dad think I'm silly for having one-sided conversations with Missy, but they don't get it. Missy listens, and I can hear in my mind what she would say.

Missy slowly swims close to the dock, her flat tail moving up and down, and her rounded flippers flapping slowly. Her calf sticks close to her, nuzzling her. Seeing this adorable new life makes me forget my school problems. "I wonder what your name is," I say. "Once I have a better idea of your personality, I'll come up with the perfect name."

VVVVROOOM. Another motorboat zooms along. These tourists are the worst. They blast by on their way to the springs to see the manatees, not caring if they hit one on the way.

But this time the boat slows way down as it approaches. It makes a wide turn and heads our way. My breathing stops. The river is pretty wide at our house, but I can't handle another close call, especially with Missy and her baby in its path.

Missy and her baby paddle away, one large and one small shape, blurring as they swim off. I sag with relief.

The boat pulls up to the dock next door. A few weeks ago, the SOLD sign showed up, and since then I've been wondering who'll move in. I had a secret hope a kid my age would move in and we could become friends. But if these people are my new neighbors, whoever they are, I can't stand them already.

I edge slowly down the dock and duck partway behind a tree. There's no way I'm going to say hello or wave to random strangers who nearly mowed down Missy and her baby. They're practically manatee murderers.

From the boat, a thin man and a girl about my age get off. Her thick brown hair flaps behind her and her spindly legs and arms remind me of a crane. The man, an older male version of her, must be her dad. She runs down the dock and heads to the house next door. "I love it, I love it!" Her voice rings shrill and loud. I cringe. Her shriek is probably the exact frequency that repels manatees and other marine mammals. Maybe someone should bottle that as a manatee warning system for boats.

Missy and her calf will never return with all that noise. If this girl's my new neighbor, her boat could run into them, and all the peace and quiet and everything amazing, including all the manatees, will disappear. My stomach knots up even more. I'll either have to talk to her or stay inside the house forever.

Everything's ruined.

I storm up the stairs to the covered porch that is Mom's studio. Mom stands in front of a dresser, holding a stiff bristle brush and running her hand through her short hair. Her studio is cluttered with unfinished furniture, shelves of paints and brushes, and random found objects.

Mom puts down the brush. "Becca bug, I didn't hear you come in. How was school?"

"I saw Missy, and she has a baby!"

"How wonderful!" With a delighted grin, Mom hustles over and gives me a hug. "It's been a while since you saw her. And a baby manatee!"

"But it's not okay." I sink into the ratty but comfy couch. "They're in danger. The boats are too fast and could hit them any moment." I hug a throw pillow, close my eyes, and inhale the scent of paint fumes and sawdust. "And then another boat came with a man and a girl. I think they're our new neighbors."

"Really? We should go over and meet them. Let's bring them cookies."

"You're missing the point! I don't want to meet them." I hate sounding like a six-year-old, but I can't help it. "Their boat could've killed Missy and her baby."

"I'm sure they were paying attention." Mom gets up. "Let's make our patented chocolate chip cookies, and we can stop by together."

I give her side-eye. I'm always up for making chocolate chip cookies, even if they're probably really patented by Nestlé since we use the recipe on the bag. It's the stopping-by-and-meeting-the-neighbors part I'm not into at all. Even the idea of scrumptious, chocolaty cookies is not enough for me to face strangers. "No thanks," I say.

Mom gives me that look, all narrow eyes and slightly sad, as if she's wondering where she got a daughter like me. Still, she says brightly, "Let's go ahead and make cookies anyway."

"Fine." I know she thinks getting me in a good cookie-baking mood will change my mind, but I'm one step ahead of her. Getting me in a good cookie-baking mood will only result in a great cookie-eating session.

When we bake, it's mostly me doing the work and Mom keeping me company, drinking iced tea and scrolling for new ideas on her phone. Her latest project is giving a flea market dresser distressed and beachy vibes. Ha. Her customers sure would be distressed if they found out how little Mom actually paid for the "eclectic chic" pieces they buy from her. She'll ask me for my opinions and sometimes she even takes my ideas and turns them into something cool, like the time she stamped flamingos all over an old mirror.

My thoughts turn back to Missy and her baby. I pull out the baking sheet, bowl, and mixer with a clatter, slamming the cabinet door.

"What's the matter, Becca?"

"I'm worried about the danger of boats hitting manatees." I put the butter in the microwave to soften it and jab at the timer. I can't believe Mom doesn't get it. "It's not fair. Manatees are the gentlest creatures in the ocean. A manatee has never been seen fighting, not in captivity or in the wild.

They'd never hurt anyone. If people were more like manatees, the world would be a better place."

"You have a kind heart, Becca," Mom says. "I bet you can figure out a way to make a difference for those manatees."

Me, make a difference? I can't even talk to cashiers. Or kids at school. Or anyone not in my family.

But Missy can't speak for herself at all. Neither can her calf.

I measure the flour and other dry ingredients. I'm totally useless at talking to strangers, but maybe there's another way. "What do you think if I make some signs to tell boats to slow down?"

"Aren't there already minimum wake signs in the river?"

"Not around here. I could use your neon paints from when you did those retro chairs."

"That's a great idea." A crafty look steals over Mom's face. "Let's make a deal. I'll let you use my paints if you come with me to meet the neighbors."

My stomach roils at the thought. I sense a humiliation waiting to happen, but I square my shoulders. Saving Missy and her friends is what's important. I'll go meet the neighbors—I just won't promise to actually talk to them. "Fine."

I spend the rest of cookie-making thinking about the signs. I could draw a really cute baby manatee and write, SLOW DOWN, BABY IN THE WATER. Or have a manatee pointing angrily at the boaters: WE WANT YOU TO SLOW DOWN or NO MANATEE MAULINGS ALLOWED.

While the cookies bake, I scribble sketches on a scrap of paper.

"All right, the cookies are cool enough. Let's go meet our neighbors," Mom says. "After quality control, of course." She winks and bites into a cookie.

I was hoping she'd forget about our deal. But, nope. Her mind's a steel trap. I eat two cookies and move as slowly as I can, but we still end up on our neighbors' doorstep, me holding a plate of gooey, warm cookies, Mom ringing the bell.

The door opens and the man from the boat greets us with a half smile and quizzical look.

"Hi, I'm Allison Wong," Mom says. "We live next door. Welcome to the neighborhood." She nudges me.

I hand the cookies over, and my gaze darts to the ground. Good thing my tan hides my flushed face.

"This is my daughter, Becca." Mom cuts me a disappointed glance. Sometimes I feel like I need to introduce myself to her. *Hello, Mom, meet your daughter, Becca, the girl who doesn't talk to adults voluntarily.*

"Thanks. I'm Peter Carlson." His half smile stretches into a real one. *Take the cookies so we can go already,* I think. He takes the plate and turns to the house. "Amelia! Come meet our new neighbors."

Oh, great. The girl from the boat bounds to the doorway with a grin that matches her dad's. "Hi!"

"This is Becca," Mom says. I know my mom wants me to be all cheerful, and I'm embarrassing her by standing here mute. I glance at the girl and give her a queasy smile. Now I probably look weird, and I feel worse for even trying.

"Wanna go check out the river?" Amelia says.

My brows scrunch together. She wants *me* to check out the river? We moved here when I was seven, and I know every bend and tree stump of that shoreline.

"Go on, Becca," Mom says. I stare pleadingly at her, but she's back to chatting with her new buddy. "What brings you here, Peter?"

"This area has a lot of opportunities."

"What do you do?"

"My wife and I flip houses," he says. "We buy old homes, fix them up, and resell them or rent them on Airbnb. There are a lot of great properties along this river that just need a little TLC." I mentally roll my eyes. People who use acronyms in their conversations are very suspect.

Amelia skips by me and clatters down the steps. "Come on." She waves. Everything about her is a lot—her voice, her hyper energy, even her smile. Mom and her dad are talking house renovations now. At least going out back will take me to the river, where I might see Missy and her baby again. And maybe—hopefully—my first impression of this girl is wrong. I really want to have a human friend, and even better, one who lives right next door.

I follow Amelia, lagging behind. Her backyard is like mine, but the trees are thicker and closer together. Both our houses are on the older side, built on stilts, and set in a wild and wooded area. While a multicolored woven hammock hangs under our house, along with our paddleboards, kayaks, and a Ping-Pong table, the underside of her house is empty.

"What do you do for fun around here?" Amelia asks. Before I get a chance to open my mouth, she says, "I'm an ice-skater, but I doubt there's a lot of that here in Florida. We just moved from Baltimore. What grade are you in? I'm in sixth grade. I don't think I'm going to like coming to a new school in the middle of the year. Do you have sisters or brothers? I have two half brothers who are much older than me. They're both in college, so I'm practically an only child."

I stare at her. This is not going to work out. I'd like to lodge a complaint and return my neighbors for a refund. It would've been one thing if the girl next door had turned out to be shy, like me. A reader, maybe. A reader would've been great—we could be best friends forever and never even talk to each other. But all this girl does is talk. I should've known it wouldn't work the minute she started hollering out on the river. Serves me right for getting my hopes even half-way up.

I walk ahead to the shoreline to put some distance between us.

Amelia picks up a rock and hurls it into the water.

"Don't!" I blurt out before I even think about it, my face flushing with heat.

"Why not? It's just a rock."

"The manatees," I stammer. "They're out there. You could hit them."

"Manatees?" Amelia's eyes grow round. "Real live manatees? They look like funny hippos, right?"

"Well, sort of. Some people call them sea cows."

"Sea cows!" Amelia bursts into laughter. "Moooo!" She runs around pretending to swim-gallop, which, by the way, is not how manatees or cows move at all. She hitches her thumbs in her shorts and walks around bowlegged. "Giddyup. I'm a sea cowgirl wranglin' them darn sea cows. We're roundin' them up for the ole seaside rodeo."

I'm pretty sure my jaw unhinges.

This is all too much. Amelia is making fun of my best friend in the world. How could I ever be friends with someone who mocks manatees? I turn and run back to my house, cutting across our backyards, weaving in and out among the trees.

"Where are you going? What's wrong?"

What's wrong is this new girl moving into my backyard

and making fun of my manatee friends. The door slams behind me and I'm back home, where it's safe and quiet.

"Why did you run off like that earlier today?" Mom asked, her voice laced with concern.

We're at the table, Mom, Dad, and me. Between making cookies and meeting our new neighbors, Mom didn't have time to cook, so Dad brought home the usual from Publix—rotisserie chicken, mac 'n' cheese, and sweet tea. It's one of my favorite dinners aside from my Grandma Popo's garlic chicken stir-fry.

I take my time chewing my food. "I don't know. I wanted to get home."

Mom and Dad exchange glances. It's their *worried about our daughter's social skills* look. I'm aware I lack them, thank you very much. Now they're either going to launch into their talk about how I need to stop caring about what other people think, or they're going to pretend everything's okay.

"So you said they renovate houses?" Dad asks. Pretending, it is. "Did you tell them how you refurbish old furniture?"

"Yes." Mom perks up. "I'm going to meet his wife tomorrow

for coffee. I have some great ideas for helping them furnish their renovated homes. I think this could be the beginning of a nice partnership."

"It's great we're getting some forward-thinking people moving here," Dad says. "I've always thought this is an underrated area. It's beautiful and a great place for people to buy second homes or come visit. Tourism is the key. Communities have to grow or they die."

"I like it the way it is," I mutter into my mac 'n' cheese. Dad grew up here and moved away after high school but came back to start his own business and to be closer to Grandma after Grandpa died. He never stops reminding us about how much he misses big-city life, even though I know he loves the water as much as I do. Kayaking with Grandma on the river is my favorite activity, but motorboats are Dad's thing. At least he watches out for manatees in the water and pays attention to the rules, unlike other people. More loudly, I say, "What about the manatees?"

"What about them?" Dad asks.

"If more people come here, they're going to be in more danger."

Dad leans back. "It's a tough dilemma. I'm all for nature and protecting animals, but people should come first. A town like this has to keep its young people from moving away. You know, I'm helping the chamber of commerce organize a winter festival to bring tourists to the area."

"Have you picked a theme yet?" Mom says.

"We thought about a music festival or a fishing derby but decided on a boating festival."

My face grows hot. Dad sells and rents boats and motor craft, so he's always trying to find new customers. It figures he's planning the festival to help promote his business. But now it hits me—he's part of the bigger problem. The more boats he sells, the more manatees will be in danger of being mowed down.

I put down my fork, my chicken suddenly ashy and tasteless.

"I'm looking forward to it," Dad says. "Maybe our new neighbor—did you say his name was Peter?—can help bring new energy to the project."

Reviving the town sounds good, but there's something that bothers me about his line of thinking. Like, what's the point of coming to live in a paradise if you're just going to ruin it? The manatees matter too.

3

"Hi, Becca." Amelia stands at the bus stop with her backpack by her feet.

I stumble, and my heart promptly shrivels into a dark pit. I forgot she'd be going to my school. Or maybe I was in denial. "Hi," I stammer.

"Why did you bug out like that yesterday?"

I bend down and root through my backpack. I wasn't *trying* to be rude. I'm just bad with people. I want to tell her how much the manatees mean to me, how her jokes made me so angry, and how the thought of her boat and loud, careless ways will change everything. But I don't have the courage to tell her any of this. I finally look up. "The manatees that come by our dock— Your boat scared them off, and . . ." My voice trails off. I'm so tongue-tied I can't even explain myself.

Amelia's eyes widen. "I'm sorry. I didn't realize." Her apology seems so genuine that it's hard to be mad at her. Something loosens in me.

It's probably my turn to apologize, but I'm not sure. "I'm sorry I ran away without explaining." My face heats up, but Amelia smiles.

When the yellow bus for Diamond Springs Middle School pulls up, a familiar pit of dread kicks in as I think about being invisible again. Except today all the kids stare out the window at Amelia, the new girl. They stare at me too, because I'm getting on the bus with her. I sit in my usual seat, an empty one three rows from the front, far from the cool kids in the back. Amelia glances around the bus. The other kids give her curious looks. She's living my exact worst nightmare—being the center of attention of a group of semi-hostile strangers. Except for some reason, Amelia's smiling widely.

Next thing I know, she plops down next to me. Oh. Now everyone's paying attention to *us*. But a part of me warms up. I've never had someone who sits next to me like it's normal. She's too new to know that she's supposed to ignore me.

"Tell me more about the manatees," she says. "I looked for them after you left, but I didn't see anything in the water."

I shift toward her. My heart goes into double time. It's so hard to open up, but thinking about Missy makes it easier. "What do you want to know?"

"Everything! What's the best thing about them?"

I could go on and on. There's so much to love. How gentle they are. Their cute faces with their button eyes and short, whiskery snouts. Except I can't, because she might think I'm weird. I finally say, "They're herbivores, which means they only eat plants." Ugh. What a dumb thing to say. I'm sure she knows what an herbivore is.

"I think it's special when an animal won't kill another to survive," Amelia says.

I sit up straighter. This girl might not be so terrible after all. She's got a good heart, which is a promising sign for a potential friend. "Right? They're really gentle giants."

"Next time we're on manatee lookout, I'll be real quiet," she says. "I've always wanted to see something special in the wild. At the Baltimore Aquarium, there are so many cool sea creatures. I love the jellyfish and the sharks."

I purse my lips. "I hate aquariums. It's depressing to see animals in glass cages."

Amelia flinches, and I realize how judgy I sound. Why did I have to blurt that out and sound so mean? I'm so bad at this making-friends business.

She frowns. "I never thought about it that way. I love learning about animals. It makes me want to protect them and love them more."

My heart sinks. She's the first person in a long time who's tried to be friendly and I go and act like a jerk. No wonder people ignore me. I don't know what to say to get the conversation back on track, so I sink into silence for the rest of the trip to school.

School is pretty much the usual, where I keep to myself and get my work done. Amelia and I don't cross paths because we have separate schedules, except for science. It's not my favorite because Ms. Amato is too energetic. She's always doing stuff like zooming around to demonstrate an elliptical orbit or having kids reenact plate tectonics. Even though it's entertaining, it gets exhausting, because I'm always worried about being called on.

I sit down and line my book up on my desk, but the girls around me are still laughing and talking. "Homeostasis," Ms. Amato says, which quiets the class. "Let's get started. For the next couple of months, you will work in groups of three on a project for the science fair. I'll hand out a packet that goes over the rules. You can pick almost any topic, as long as you use the scientific method or rely on primary research. You'll give oral presentations, and your final project will be a display."

A mix of groans and excited murmurs fills the room. My heart is squeezed in a vise, and my head throbs. I'm not sure which is worse—the oral presentation, or the fact I'll have to work with others.

"Your partners are listed on the whiteboard." Ms. Amato clicks on the screen and the names of everyone in the class are grouped in threes. My group pops up: Amelia Carlson, Becca Wong Walker, and Deion Williams.

"Get together with your group, and I'll give you the rest of the period to brainstorm topics. I'll walk around and answer any questions."

I'm not sure what to think. Amelia's starting to grow on me, but she might be mad at me for putting down her love of aquariums on the bus. Deion is the class clown who finds a joke in everything. I doubt he even knows who I am. My single scarring memory of him was in fourth grade when he hocked a disgusting glob of spit into the air and then caught it with his mouth and swallowed it.

Amelia and I are sitting near each other, so we scoot our desks together. Deion scrapes a desk over with a smile. I can't tell if he's about to be friendly or make fun of us.

"It's my lucky day," Deion says. "I get to work with Becca, the mystery girl who's so quiet we don't know if she can talk, and I'm paired with the new girl too."

I stare at him. It seems like he's trying to be funny, but it's not really ha-ha funny. It's more like *that's weird* funny. I don't like the idea that he's thought about me enough to decide that I'm strange.

"I'm Amelia, from Baltimore," Amelia says. "I've got some ideas. I've always wanted to learn about dreams. We should keep a dream journal and track our dreams for a month and figure out if our dreams have anything to do with our regular lives. Or if they're prophetic. Like, sometimes I swear I'm psychic. Have you ever had these weird dreams about penguins, for example, and then the next day you see a penguin meme? I mean, that's totally a sign that I'm supernaturally connected to the world."

"Dreams?" Deion raises an eyebrow. "Dude, that's weird."

I flinch even though he's talking to Amelia. What if he shoots down my ideas?

"You've got a better idea?" Amelia says, arching her own eyebrow. It's like I'm watching an eyebrow-raising duel. I can't believe his insult doesn't faze her at all.

"Yeah. I'm a swimmer, right?"

Huh. I had no idea he was a swimmer. That's really cool. I'd like to ask him about it, but he keeps talking without taking a breath and, of course, I don't have the courage to interrupt him.

"Let's go around and time how long everyone can hold their breath and find out whether or not they do sports, and if so, what kind of sports they do." He leans forward. "I think swimmers have the best lung capacity and can hold their breath the longest. We can compare different sports."

"That's not science," Amelia says.

Actually, it is science, but I keep my mouth shut.

"And dream journals are?" Deion says.

"Okay, if we don't do dream journals, let's pick a body part and learn all about it. Like eyes," she says. "My uncle's an ophthalmologist. We can make a big eye out of a Styrofoam ball and label it. We could come up with some kind of vision experiment, like, I don't know, comparing how people see colors."

"I know," Deion says. "Let's make one of those volcano science projects, but inside of a giant eye. We'll make an exploding eyeball." He doubles over the desk laughing, cracking himself up.

This is exactly how every group project goes. Everyone comes up with ideas, it degenerates into silliness, and eventually someone bosses the others into submission. No one'll work on the project until a few days before it's due and I won't be able to bring myself to remind them, so I'll end up doing most of the work. I don't know why teachers make us do group projects. It's not something I'm ever going to do in my other dream job, where I get to work in an underwater submersible, all by myself, never having to talk to anyone again.

But. But. Missy and her calf keep coming to mind. I can't abandon them. They really need some help, and this could be a way to do something. We could research what will help them the most, or we could make signs together. Heat rushes through me as I open my mouth to chime in. My palms grow clammy and my breath goes shallow.

"Manatees," I manage to say.

"Exploding eyeballs, that's ridiculous," Amelia says.

"What'd you say?" Deion says.

I gulp like a goldfish. "Manatees." My voice sounds reedy. "Let's study manatees and how we can help them."

Amelia and Deion both look at me, and I cringe inside. They're probably thinking how stupid the idea is. Or how weird I am.

Amelia nods slowly. "Manatees come by the river in our backyards. We could totally observe them."

"I still like my eyeball idea," Deion says. "What's so great about manatees?"

My heart goes into overdrive. I'm never going to convince him when I can barely talk to him. I tried talking with Amelia on the bus, but that didn't turn out well. I take a breath. "Manatees are super interesting." I sputter out the first thing that comes to mind. "The manatees' closest living relatives are elephants. Old-timey sailors thought they were mermaids."

Deion laughs. "They must've had pretty bad eyesight."

I smile but cringe inside. I need him on board, not laughing at a joke. I search for something else to say. "There's this one manatee who comes to my house. Her name is Missy and she has a new baby." I swallow hard. "If we research the dangers manatees face, we can help protect them. I can't stand the idea of them getting hurt."

He looks at me intently, as if he's never seen me before. I glance away, unused to being the center of attention. He probably thinks I'm strange to be so into manatees. "I guess manatees are cool," Deion says.

"Let's do it," Amelia says.

I can't believe what I'm hearing. I said my piece and didn't sink through the floor. Better yet, they listened to me and like my idea! I let out a wobbly whoosh of air, relief and excitement washing over me.

We have a topic and it might even help Missy and her new baby.

4

A week's gone by since Ms. Amato announced the science project, and we need to come up with our specific project idea by tomorrow.

I hurry-walk down the aisle of the bus, keeping my head low, because Deion is getting off with Amelia and me, and the other kids must be wondering what this wiry kid, full of energy, is doing with the new girl and the weirdo. It doesn't seem like Deion or Amelia care, though, because they're chatting like old friends.

We're meeting at Amelia's house to figure out our project. I've spent plenty of time thinking about how to protect Missy and her baby and the other manatees, but we never got around to talking about it. When Amelia suggested meeting at her house after school, I was both relieved and stressed. Relieved because they weren't coming to my house but stressed wondering how I'll talk to them for a whole afternoon.

We clamber off into the warmth of the day. I love early spring, with its perfect weather, which is unlike summer, when we practically swim through a soup of heat and humidity.

"You're so lucky to live on the river and these cool houses on stilts!" Deion beelines it toward the water behind our houses.

"Let's go inside and get a snack first," Amelia says.

We follow Amelia up the steps to her house. Inside, the layout is similar to ours, with an open family room and windows overlooking the water through the tall trees, but hers is mostly empty, other than a few pieces of furniture and stacks of moving boxes. It's almost a relief to see blank walls instead of the explosion of flea market and beachcombing finds we have scattered around our place.

We head to the kitchen, where Amelia rummages through the fridge until she triumphantly holds up a box of cantaloupe cubes. She hands out forks.

"These are my favorite." Deion stabs a couple of pieces and shoves them in his mouth. "I could eat fruit at every meal," he says with his mouth full, letting the juices dribble down his chin.

I love fruit too. Sometimes I think I could be a fruitarian, but then I'd miss my bologna sandwiches. I almost say this out loud but take a bite of cantaloupe instead.

"Mmm, me too." Amelia grins.

Deion smiles back while finishing his mouthful.

My stomach squeezes into a knot. In the time it took me to wonder whether I should chime in, the two are competing to see how many cubes of cantaloupe they can stuff into their mouths, while laughing and snorting.

Raised voices from the den interrupt them. I recognize Amelia's dad's voice.

"How many times do I have to tell you not to trust the first quote you get?"

"Stop treating me like an idiot." That must be her mom, her voice filled with bitterness.

Amelia's face reddens. "Let's go outside," she mumbles.

I don't meet her eyes. Deion and I both pretend we didn't just hear her parents fighting.

I check to make sure my phone is handy. I never know

when Missy or another manatee might show up, and I'll need to record them. As we head down to the river, the *plap plap* of the water lapping at the bank soothes me. The cypress trees with their gnarled roots standing sentry in the river push away any thoughts of Amelia's parents.

The dock creaks as I walk out and sit on the edge, dangling my legs and enjoying the slight breeze. Amelia sits down nearby, while Deion scampers up and down the dock like a gecko. Amelia gazes at the water below her feet, her body hunched over. I want to make her feel better, but I don't know how.

"Should we get to work on our ideas?" I say.

She sighs. "Sure. Deion, come over here. We've got work to do."

Deion lopes over and scoots down next to us. "Okay, geniuses. Or is it genii? What should we do?"

"I don't think it's genii. That would make us jinns or spirits," Amelia says. "Anyway, you're assuming a lot to think you're in the company of more than one genius." She winks at me. "Hey, why did you curl up like that?"

I must've tucked my chin into my chest at her words. I'm

not used to her friendly joking. I don't understand how Deion and Amelia are so easy with each other when they've just met. I wish I could joke around like that, not worrying what they might think about me. I look out to the river. "The manatees are in trouble with the boats. We should—"

Before I can finish my thought, Deion jumps in. "We should measure the lung capacity of manatees!" His eyes light up and he throws an air punch. "If they could hold their breaths longer, manatees wouldn't need to come up for air as often, and they'd be hit by boats less."

"How're we going to do that?" Amelia says. "Let's make a Styrofoam sculpture of a manatee or a scene of a manatee getting hit by a boat." Her eyes widen. "Or we can create a puppet show about manatees."

"Are you in love with Styrofoam?" Deion says.

"No, but you are with your breathing experiments." Amelia scoffs.

"An experiment is better than a model."

"A model that teaches is better than an experiment we can't do. How're you going to get a manatee to cooperate with us?"

I stare at both of them with increasing dismay. I was right to worry when I got paired with them. Deion doesn't take anything seriously, and Amelia is weirdly obsessed with Styrofoam. Their conversation makes me want to fold in like origami. I want to speak up, but I can't.

The water ripples with the distinctive circles of an approaching—

"Manatee!" I point. "A manatee is coming our way."

Amelia and Deion stop bickering, and we scramble to our feet. The circles of water move our way, and the dark shape of a manatee appears. Even though I've seen plenty of manatees, each time I encounter one fills me with awe. Their slow grace as they move through the water, going about their day, not caring about us people, reminds me of the vastness of the world. The three of us, standing on the dock, with the sky above, river below, and greenery all around, and the manatee, a friendly soul—all make up a whole lot of wonderful.

I glance over at Amelia and Deion and see a bit of the same feeling in their faces.

"There's a little one next to it!" Amelia grips my arm. "Oh, Becca, I can't believe I'm actually seeing them."

"It's Missy and her baby." My grin spills into my voice. "Hiya, girl. What a cool mama you are."

Missy swims closer, like she's saying hi. Her baby hangs back, probably unsure about us humans. Once this baby gets to know us, I bet it'll be just as friendly as its mom.

"Missy, I'd like you to meet Amelia and Deion, my . . . classmates." I glance over at them and feel my face grow warm. I almost called them my friends, but I don't know them well enough to say that. But I'd really like to be friends with them, I think. They don't seem to notice my awkward pause.

I wake my phone and start to record.

"It's Missy the manatee and her very cute offspring," Deion intones into the camera. He waves at me to record him.

Even though it's against policy—I mean, I'm the narrator of my videos, but how can I resist his eager expression?—I turn the camera on him and make sure Missy and her calf are in the frame. Half of Deion's face is off-screen, but that's okay, the manatees are the stars.

"Deion Williams, nature reporter for the, er . . ." He pauses and tilts his head up, as if to find inspiration in the clouds.

"Manatee Mammal Network, where it's all things manatee, twenty-four seven. Today's magnificent specimen is Missy and her baby. Such a cute little one, with, I'm sure, great lung capacity."

I giggle, making my phone wobble. Deion's not so bad after all.

Amelia squeezes into the frame. Her and Deion's heads fill up most of the screen, with Missy and her calf vague blobs in the background. She smiles widely. "Mr. Williams, thank you for the intro. Amelia Carlson, award-winning MMN reporter. We now turn to an expert on manatees who can tell us why you, the watcher of this show, should care about these adorable creatures." Amelia takes the phone out of my hands and turns it on me, shuffling me around so she can video the manatees too.

My heart leaps. My stomach roils. A clash of two worlds. When I do my private videos, my words flow, especially when I talk about Missy. But when I'm with other people, I worry about every word that comes out of my mouth.

I glance back at Missy and her baby. Missy is still on the bottom of the river, and her baby has its snout under her flipper. It's nursing! Missy is so patient, not eating, just hanging out, while the baby's tucked under her armpit. My heart fills. I want to talk about what a treasure manatees are. From the point of view of evolution, they shouldn't exist. They're slow and tubby, but they don't have any natural enemies. It's as if all the other animals took a look at them and decided these creatures are too kind to kill. Only people are careless enough to hurt the manatees.

But none of that comes out of my mouth. My face warms up. I reach for my phone. "Let's just take videos of them."

Deion leans over the dock and looks at the pair with wide eyes.

Amelia hands me my phone with a curious look. "How about we name the baby manatee?"

I've wanted to be the one to name the baby, but it's kind of cool to do it together. Somehow it means more with the two of them helping come up with a name. "We need to give it a good name," I say.

Deion ponders the baby. "How about Sunny or Happy?" For once, it doesn't seem like he's cracking a joke. "You know, because he's like a ray of light."

My smile widens. "Sunny's a good name."

"How do you know it's a he?" Amelia asks.

"We don't," Deion says. "That's why Sunny's a great name. It works for either a girl or a boy. Sunny!" He hustles to the edge of the dock and waves his arms wildly. "Sunny! Having a good meal?"

Missy and Sunny move apart and swim away.

I shoot Deion a dirty look.

"You scared them away," Amelia says.

"I'm sorry," Deion says. "They're so cool." His look of genuine joy makes it hard for me to stay mad at him. Seems he's got a heart underneath that jokey exterior after all.

My own heart is full of love for Missy and Sunny, but I feel weighed down with a bag full of worries. How are we going to help these two?

I actually groan out loud when I wake up. In the commotion of spotting Missy and Sunny yesterday, we never agreed on our specific topic, which is due today.

On the bus to school, Amelia says, "Becca, I can't get over seeing my first manatee—and a baby too. I'm glad we picked out a name, and I'm not sure I agree with Deion that it's a boy, but I guess it doesn't matter too much. I'll have to look into how to tell the difference."

My hands grow clammy. I'm getting used to her paragraph-long statements, and I'm starting to like her, but trying to have an actual back-and-forth conversation still makes me nervous. Especially when I'm about to push back. "We need to come up with our specific project."

Amelia smiles. "Don't worry. I'll take care of it."

I wonder what she means and want to press her about it, but my mouth clamps shut. We're just starting to be friends, so I better not mess it up by pushing her. I wish I had some of her confidence. I'd buy some of it if it came in a bottle.

It's fifth period and Ms. Amato calls each group up to her desk to explain our projects. I fiddle with my mechanical pencil, tapping it against the desktop. I wish I knew more Morse code than DOT DOT DOT, DASH DASH DASH, DOT DOT DOT, which everyone knows is "SOS." But on second thought, *Save Our Ship* is all I need to know right now.

Deion, Amelia, and I walk up to Ms. Amato, who looks up over her square glasses, her curly brown hair springing like baby fern fronds. "Amelia, Deion, and Becca. What do you have for me?"

Amelia looks at me, then Deion. Deion looks at Amelia. I keep my eyes fixed on Ms. Amato's laptop. Why isn't Amelia speaking up? She said she had it taken care of.

Deion clears his throat. "We, er . . . decided to study the . . ."

Amelia interrupts him. ". . . the eyeballs of manatees, no, I mean . . ."

". . . the lung capacity . . ." Deion says as Amelia jostles him into me.

I always thought wishing for the earth to open up and swallow someone whole was a cliché, but it turns out this is an actual feeling.

Ms. Amato looks at us sharply and turns to me. "Becca, does your group have a project or not?"

My mouth is so dry. Why is she asking me? "We haven't completely figured it out yet," I stammer, "but it'll have to do with manatees."

"What about manatees?"

"We're figuring it out," Deion says hopefully.

Our teacher looks like a disappointed mama bird who found out her baby birds can't fly. "I'm going to have to give you an incomplete. You have until Monday to give me your topic or I'll have to give you a zero." She reaches into a file folder and pulls out the dreaded yellow slips. "I need each of your parents to sign this." She scribbles the date and a note on each slip. My vision goes gray for a brief moment. I've never had a homework demerit before. What am I going to tell Mom and Dad?

We shuffle back to our seats. I glance at Amelia, who doesn't seem too bothered. She said not to worry on the bus, but it turns out she had no ideas. It seems she's too flaky to be counted on. Deion doesn't seem worried either as he goes off to sit by some boys huddled over a tablet. We're allowed to use them to make quizlets and school-related things, but I bet they're looking up basketball scores.

Amelia and I head back to our seats.

"Becca, what are we going to do?"

I take a deep breath and exhale. I want to confront her and ask her why she said she had a plan when she didn't, but I can't bring myself to do it. I do know I have to speak up for Missy and for my grades. "Well," I start slowly, "one of the biggest threats to manatees is they're getting hit by boats, because boaters don't pay attention and manatees are slow swimmers."

"So what do we do?" Amelia asks. "Jump up and down and yell at them?"

"I've been thinking about making signs."

"But that's not a science project. Don't we need to figure out something experimental, come up with a hypothesis?"

"Let me check." My face warms as I pull out the folder with the guidelines. "Here, it says we can develop educational materials, but we have to use primary research."

"Primary research?"

I read on. "Primary research is when you collect information directly from the world or interviews, and not just from books."

"Signs wouldn't be primary research," Amelia says.

My shoulders wilt. She's right. I can make signs on my own, but we still need to come up with a specific science project.

I can't give up. I'll just have to work extra hard to think of a better idea.

After school, I head to the dock. I hope Missy's there so we can talk. It's been too long since I've confided in her. The leaves of the old oaks sway in the breeze, stray leaves stuttering into the water.

I pace up and down the dock, keeping my eyes peeled for signs of Missy or Sunny. Falling behind before our project even begins is a horrible feeling, and I have to show Mom and Dad my homework demerit. I hate having to depend on Amelia and Deion. It's Friday afternoon, and once again, we made no plans to figure out our assignment over the weekend.

On the bus home, I researched manatees on my phone. My stomach churns remembering what I read. One article showed a dead manatee floating upside down in a canal, its tail caught in a net and its body sickly green. Another talked about manatees dying from getting cold-stunned in the winter and falling sick from red tide algae. The biggest killer of manatees in northwest Florida is boat strikes.

All the info is out there, but I'm not sure how to make educational materials out of primary sources. The thought of interviewing someone is paralyzing.

I look out over the river. A white heron wings its way low across the water, no boats in sight.

A series of ripples shows up. It's manatee time! I break into a grin and get to my feet.

Missy swims over with Sunny by her side. I don't know whether Sunny is male or female, but I've started to think of Sunny as a boy. Sunny is only a few weeks old, but he's just as graceful as Missy, sticking close to his mom. Missy nibbles at the eelgrass by our dock. Sunny turns his small, trusting face to me. I swear he's smiling at me.

"Sunny," I say softly, "your mom has been such a good friend. I can tell you'll be a great listener too."

I turn to Missy. "Missy, you have no idea what a week it's been." My pent-up words spill out. "I was so excited when Amelia and Deion agreed to work on manatees, but they went off on their own ideas, and now I don't know how to get them to focus. It's the first time since forever that I feel like I'm making friends, but I'm so bad at it."

Missy doesn't answer, but I know she understands. She munches away on the eelgrass so she can make milk for a calf so adorable all I want to do is jump into the river and hug him.

The two move away from the dock, back to the middle of the river.

A splash catches my eye. Down the river, a fin and slice of dark gray pops up and down in the water, heading toward the manatees. A moment later, it comes up again.

A dolphin!

I've never seen a dolphin this far inland before. The dorsal fin and the sleek shiny body break the surface again, this time right near Missy and Sunny. It's so frisky, popping up and down.

If Missy or Sunny are scared or bothered, I can't tell. They don't seem to mind this playful dolphin. It even jumps partway out of the water, sprinkling rainbow droplets. It swims fast and spins, brimming with joy and life.

The dolphin disappears beneath the water. I scan the river, waiting for it to come up again. I look around. I can't believe no one else is here to see this dolphin and its antics. It's as if I've been given a secret gift—something rare, just for me. I feel so special.

The dolphin doesn't come back, and Missy and Sunny move away. The river is once again smooth and placid. Did I imagine this strange and wonderful event? Too late, I realize I didn't record it.

The dolphin showing up was so incredible I can't wait to tell Mom and Dad about it. But if it wasn't captured on video, no one will believe me.

6

I kick my shoes off at the doorway and head toward the chopping noises in the kitchen. "Mom, a dolphin's out in the river, playing with the manatees."

"Really?" Mom looks up from chopping scallions. "I've never heard of a dolphin coming this far inland. Was it sick?"

"I don't think so. It was really playful, jumping out of the water."

Mom puts down the knife and wipes her hands on a kitchen towel. "Let's check it out." We go to her studio-porch, which overlooks the river, and Mom picks up the binoculars. After a moment, she shakes her head. "I don't see anything, but how wonderful. I'll keep an eye out for it when I'm working. Come help me with the food."

"What's for dinner?" Mom doesn't cook much, but when

she does, it's something yummy like my Grandma Popo's Chinese ribs. I'm guessing it won't be stir-fry tonight because the rice cooker isn't on.

"Dad's bringing home takeout," Mom says. "This is for tomorrow. We're having the Carlsons and Grandma over for an afternoon barbecue. Why don't you help me with this teriyaki steak marinade?"

At the mention of Amelia's parents coming over, a queasy feeling comes over me. At her house, I was so uncomfortable hearing her parents fight. I can't picture spending a whole afternoon with them. Back at the kitchen, I wash my hands and gather the cooking wine and garlic from the fridge and the soy sauce and the sugar from the pantry.

"You and Amelia seem to be getting along nicely." Mom scoops the scallions into a ziplock bag. She adds some chopped garlic from the jar and reaches for the sugar. "What did I tell you? All you need to do to make some friends is be your wonderful self and not worry so much. Get out of your head, you know?"

I don't know what to say. I hate it when Mom and Dad act like everything will be fine if I only try harder or don't worry or try being myself. It's not that easy. I would get out of my head if I could. It's not all that fun in there. I don't even know what this supposed wonderful self is.

As I feel my face about to crumple, Mom's expression softens. She reaches over and gives me a forearm hug, holding out her marinade-y hands. "Becca bug, I know it's hard for you to make new friends. I'm really proud you're making the effort with Amelia and Deion."

A rush of gratitude washes over me. Mom isn't perfect, but she's trying too. I vow to suck it up and get through tomorrow's barbecue.

"Help me with the rest of this," she says.

I take the soy sauce and white wine, shake some into the bag, and mush the whole thing around. This is my favorite part of marinating things.

"Mom," I say, "remember our deal?"

"What deal?"

"You said I could use your paints to make signs if I met the neighbors. I think I've done way more than that."

Mom laughs. "You're right. Put this in the fridge, and I'll help you with the signs. You'll probably want to use something sturdier than poster board."

After we clean up, we head to her studio. I know we can't make signs for our science project, but I have to do something to make a difference. I remember the homework demerit and my stomach scrunches in on itself. "Mom, I got a yellow homework slip."

She gives me a sharp look. "That's unlike you. What happened?"

"We were supposed to come up with our specific project by today, but it didn't happen." I quickly add, "Ms. Amato said we won't get a zero on this part if we come up with an idea by Monday."

"Dad and I can help you think of a project." Mom frowns. "But you need a consequence if you don't keep up your grade in science. You have to take these projects seriously. I'll talk about it with Dad."

I do take this project seriously. I need to do well not just for my grade but for Missy and Sunny too. I have to do everything I can to help my manatee friends, and both the project and making signs are ways to help them. Mom and I pull out the corrugated plastic and paints for the signs. Maybe I'll draw a dolphin on the sign too.

I push away my nagging thoughts about what kind of consequences Mom and Dad will come up with. I don't want to be grounded or lose my phone, especially with so much to do to help the manatees.

It's Saturday afternoon and Amelia and I are setting the patio table on the deck. Amelia's parents are chatting with Mom, while Dad ferries the teriyaki steak from the grill. Grandma walks up from her truck parked out front, holding a casserole dish.

"What's happening, Becca?" She smiles at me with Dad's eyes, her short brown hair ruffling in the breeze.

"You're happening, Grandma." I grin and help her with the dish, peeking at the bean salad. Grandma's in her late sixties, but you wouldn't know it by the way she bustles around, does yard work, and hikes and kayaks with her friends.

After Dad introduces her to the Carlsons, they talk while Amelia and I chase after a green tree frog. I sneak a peek at her as we stalk a giant iguana. She smiles and copies my exaggerated tiptoeing, and we break into giggles. I can't believe I'm making a friend. I can't stop my giddy grin.

When we sit and eat, Mom gushes, "This salad is delicious, Marcie. I wouldn't have thought to put strawberries in a green salad."

Amelia's mom laughs. "It's my philosophy on most things. Pair unusual things together, and you get something magical." Mrs. Carlson is one of those moms who look like they always have it together and are never frazzled. Her hair is soft and pretty, and she looks ready for an Insta shoot, completely different from what I imagined when I only heard her angry voice at Amelia's. She's very different from Mom in her casual shorts and T-shirt, but they seem to get along great.

"That's my creative aesthetic too," Mom says. She and Mrs. Carlson talk about the latest decorating color trends while I dig into my steak.

"Tell me about your projects upriver," Dad says to Mr. Carlson.

Amelia's dad leans back. "We bought four old houses that sit along the river and are renovating them. While we're working on a couple of them, we're renting the others as Airbnbs."

"That'll be great for the festival I'm planning," Dad says. "Upscale Airbnbs will be a draw for tourists."

"What's the festival about?" Mrs. Carlson asks.

"We're trying to get younger, more active visitors to come to the area, so I proposed a festival of water sports, like wakeboarding, tubing, and flyboarding—like the X Games of boating."

This is the first time I've heard this part of the plan. When he said a boating festival, I didn't imagine people zooming around on the water, possibly ramming into Missy and her friends.

"That sounds great," Mr. Carlson says. "That's just the kind of thing that would appeal to younger people here. I'd love to do more than just develop a few Airbnbs. Did you hear about the new toll road the state's approved from Tampa? That'll create infrastructure for larger projects like condos."

"Which I don't agree with," Amelia's mom interjects. "We don't need huge levels of development in this area."

Her dad cuts her mom a sharp look. "I wouldn't say condos are huge levels of development."

Mrs. Carlson narrows her eyes. "You wouldn't say a lot of things."

Grandma chimes in. "I can see what Marcie's saying. This

area is truly unique—it's part of an old Florida that's disappearing." A wistful look flits across her face. "I remember when it was more wild and not a bunch of streets dotted with strip malls."

Mom glances at Dad. "I agree we want development, but it's a matter of what kind." She offers up a plate. "Would you like some corn?"

"Anyone want another drink?" Dad stands up and heads to the cooler.

My insides are queasy with this talk about festivals, boats, and new roads. I want to push my chair from the table and yell, *What about the manatees?* I look to Amelia—she's not scared to speak up like I am, and she's got to be outraged too—but she's playing with her napkin, shredding it to bits.

Amelia's mom gives a small shake of her head. "Thanks, everything is delicious. Allison, will you show me your studio? I got a glimpse of those darling chairs you're refurbishing. I would love it if you'd help us decorate our Airbnbs."

"Sure." Mom stands up. "We can clean up later."

I sneak another glance at Amelia, now drumming the table

with her fingers. "Want to go down to the water to see if we can find Missy and Sunny?" I offer.

"Yeah, sure." Amelia pushes herself from the table and practically runs from it.

We head to the river, ducking under the prickly Spanish moss draped on the trees and winding between the giant old leather ferns. Amelia's kicking every other root she comes across. I try to think of something to say to cheer her up, but nothing comes to mind. I've never been in a position like this before.

I look out at the water, and a feeling of pressure, like I'm about to burst, builds up. I want to see the dolphin again, but I'm not sure how I feel about sharing that moment with Amelia. But then again, this might be the thing to change her mood. Plus, it's not fair to keep such a wonderful thing to myself.

My words tumble out. "Guess what I saw yesterday? A dolphin was playing with the manatees."

Amelia eyes grow wide. "Does that happen a lot?"

"No. I searched online last night and I couldn't find anything like it."

A slow smile slides across Amelia's face. "That's amazing.

In the first week I've been here, I've seen a manatee mom and baby, and now maybe a dolphin?"

My smile widens, and my heart blooms. I hurry to the dock. "Maybe we can see it again."

We squat on our heels as we peer into the water. It's very clear today, so we can see the eelgrass, mixed with black stringy Lyngbya algae and the occasional small fish.

Amelia squeezes my arm and points urgently about twenty yards away. "Look! Is that it?" I follow her finger.

It's the dolphin, zooming along the bottom of the river.

"Yes!" This time I remember to pull out my phone and film it. I'm not comfortable doing my spiel in front of Amelia, so I think it in my head. *Becca Wong Walker here. We have a dolphin sighting in the upper reaches of the river, far from the Gulf of Mexico. She's a beauty—so sleek and fast.*

The dolphin holds something in its beak, which it leaves on the sandy bottom. It swims away, and I zoom in, but I can't tell what it is.

Amelia taps me excitedly on the shoulder and points. Missy and Sunny are here too! They move sedately toward us. I turn the camera to them.

Now the dolphin swims back into view, picks up the thing on the bottom of the river, and drops it next to the manatees. It's a conch shell. The dolphin darts away.

Amelia and I grip each other, both of us grinning wildly and bouncing up and down. I turn off the video, because at this point, it's a big shaking mess.

"I'm going to hyperventilate," Amelia whispers. "It left them a present."

"It's amazing. They're really friends." Missy doesn't seem to notice, but Sunny nudges the shell with his snout. He slowly turns in the direction the dolphin went and flaps his flippers, like he wants to follow. After venturing out a bit, he returns and sticks close to his mama.

In the middle of the river, the dolphin's fin breaks the surface. Moments later, the dolphin leaps into the air and spins, droplets of water arcing through the air, leaving a rainbow spray.

The water quiets, and the dolphin's gone.

Missy and Sunny slowly swim away from our dock.

Amelia and I hug each other. All traces of sadness have left her face. I'm sure my grin mirrors her ear-to-ear smile. "I can't believe how close that dolphin got, and how it was trying to be friends with Missy and Sunny. What a show-off." She continues on in a long breathless speech, which I slowly tune out, enjoying the music of her voice and the bubbly vibes she sends out to the universe.

7

It's Monday at lunch, twenty-five minutes before science, and Amelia, Deion, and I hold a panic-pick-our-project meeting. I'm thrilled to be sitting at a table with them and taking part in the conversation, instead of lurking at the edge of a group of kids who ignore me. But it's hard to concentrate with the others' shouts and laughter and the clinking and clanking of plates, trays, forks, and cups.

"I really can't get a zero," Amelia says. "My parents are on my case. And if I do badly, that's another reason for them to get mad and fight."

"Me too. If I don't fix my grade, I can't go to the next swim meet," Deion says glumly.

"My parents too," I say. "They're going to take away my phone if I mess up again on this project." I need my phone to take videos of Missy and Sunny. It's one of the only things that calms me down.

Amelia gives us a hard look. "So you got any ideas?"

I'm not sure why she thinks it's on us when she was the one who told me not to worry about it. But of course, I don't bring it up.

"Don't look at me." Deion holds up his arms like he's fending off a horde of beasts, which, come to think of it, is sort of Amelia's general energy. "I gave y'all my ideas."

"That weren't very helpful," Amelia replies. "Becca, a manatee project was your idea. What do you think we should do?"

I blink. I'm about to burst with pent-up frustration, but of course, I keep it all in. Like I always do. Up until now, I didn't know how to get Amelia and Deion to take the project seriously. Now that I've got their attention, I have no idea what to do. I've never had to be a leader in a group before.

I feel helpless and overwhelmed and need to get away. I push myself up from the table.

"Where're you going?" Deion says.

"I'm sorry, I can't—" I mumble, and take my tray to bus it.

We still have fifteen minutes until class, and I hate that I'm running away, but I can't help it. I head to Ms. Amato's class. I don't know if she'll be in the room, but I figure I can hang out there before class starts and sulk a bit. Or at least watch the sugar glider that lives in her classroom. It's a nocturnal animal, sleeping away most of the day, but seeing him hanging upside down, all tucked in, will make me feel better. To be a sugar glider, whose only job in life is to eat fruit, sleep, and look cute, sounds good about now.

I peek into Ms. Amato's room. She's sitting at her desk, eating a sandwich and typing on her laptop. I turn to go, but she must've heard me, because she turns around. "Becca, come in. What's up?"

My mouth suddenly goes dry. Running away would be too embarrassing now, so I walk into her room instead, sitting down at a desk near hers. I blink a few times and sigh. I don't want to admit we haven't come up with our topic yet, but her face is so kind and concerned.

She must have some secret magical power, because I find myself saying, "Our team is still trying to figure out our project."

"Do you have a general idea of what you want to work on?"

"We want to do something with manatees. Maybe something educational."

Ms. Amato leans back in her chair and gives me a considering look. I squirm in my seat. One of the things I hate most is being the center of attention, and I'm pinned by her stare, like a helpless moth caught by a collector. "Do you have any primary sources to develop educational materials?"

I shake my head. "We don't know any scientists studying manatees."

Ms. Amato smiles. "Well, it's your lucky day. Before teaching, I studied marine biology in graduate school and interned with the FWC. That's the Florida Fish and Wildlife Conservation Commission." She chuckles. "Don't ask me why that gets abbreviated to FWC."

I laugh nervously.

"I can try to put you in touch with someone there working on manatees. Have you done any research online?"

"I found a nonprofit group, Save the Manatee Club, that has a lot of information online."

"Check out their staff. I bet they have scientists working for them," Ms. Amato says. "You could interview someone there or at a manatee rehab center."

I nod, but my heart starts doing its pattering thing. I will not call or contact real live scientists, because it's impossible. They're adults, and strangers, two insurmountable hurdles.

Maybe Ms. Amato sees the panic in my face, because she smiles gently and says, "How did you get interested in manatees?"

I look up. "A manatee comes by my house a lot. I take videos of her, and now she has a baby."

Ms. Amato tilts her head, reminding me of a flamingo inspecting its shrimp dinner. "Videos can be primary sources too. May I see them?"

I'm about to pull out my phone to show her, but then remember they're of me in reporter mode. Even though Ms. Amato seems like she'd be understanding, I'm afraid of being seen that way. What if she thinks I'm too silly or wonders who I am to be talking about manatees? The room suddenly spins, and I need to put my head down.

"Are you okay, Becca?"

I take a deep breath. "Excuse me, I'm going to the restroom."

She gives me an awfully familiar look, like the one I see on Mom's and Dad's faces when they worry about me. "See you in class."

I give her my most lighthearted wave. "I'll be fine. Thank you, Ms. Amato." I leave the room and lean against the wall in the hallway, gulping for air.

After a few minutes, I feel better.

What she said sparks an idea. I straighten and quickly head back to the cafeteria. We have about five minutes left of lunch, and I know what to do.

I head to the table where Amelia and Deion are seated. Deion is eating a plastic cup like a goat, and the rest of the kids are laughing. I'm almost distracted by this sight, but I press forward. This is so unlike me. I would never barge in and interrupt a group of people, especially people in the middle of having fun, but Missy and Sunny and their new dolphin friend need me. And I have to do well on this project. I can't lose my phone now.

Amelia scoots over for me.

Instead of sitting, I say, "Can I talk to you two?"

Deion smiles, shrugs, and stands up with his tray. Amelia follows, and we all walk to the door.

"What's up?" Amelia asks. "Looks like your butt is on fire."

Deion snickers.

I feel my face warm up, but I'm no longer scared. "I've got an idea for our project."

"What is it? Because we need one real soon," Deion says.

"Ms. Amato said videos count as primary sources. You know how we saw the dolphin playing with the manatees?"

Amelia nods.

"You saw a dolphin playing with manatees?" Deion asks.

"It was so wild," Amelia gushes. "You should've seen it. I was there!"

"I was thinking," I say, "we should get more videos of the dolphin and the manatees."

Deion knits his brows together, then smiles. "Oh, so we're going to make a documentary or something like that?"

"Something like that." I smile back. "If we take videos of them playing and hanging around together, it'll be scientific research."

"Will it help us come up with recommendations to protect them?" Amelia asks.

Mmm. That is a good question. "I don't know."

"Maybe we'll learn something new about these animals," Amelia says.

Then the idea hits me like a blast of fireworks. "Let's make a public service ad based on our videos. That will be primary research and we'll help the manatees too."

"Like getting boats to slow down?" Amelia asks.

"Yes. Boaters need to know that their speeding boats are killing manatees, and now maybe even dolphins are in danger," I say.

Deion gives my shoulder a hearty shake. "Let's do it. You are awesome. You've saved us, just in time."

Amelia does a little jig. "I knew I was lucky to be partnered with you."

We all walk to science. They don't notice I'm walking four inches above the ground, floating through the hallways, buoyed by Amelia's smile and Deion's words. I can't believe I did that. We finally have a specific project. I won't have to let Mom and Dad down with a bad science grade, and neither will Amelia and Deion. Our video will reach more people than the signs in my backyard, and maybe we can make a difference for Missy, Sunny, and all the manatees.

8

Ms. Amato approved our idea to make a PSA based on videos of the manatees and the dolphin, so the three of us meet after school in between our other activities. Well, in between Amelia's Roller Derby classes—Florida's alternative to ice-skating, I guess—and Deion's swim practices. I don't do after-school activities, because the thought of them makes my heart do backflips. If heart palpitations counted as a sport, I'd be a superstar.

We meet at my house. We've silently agreed to avoid Amelia's house.

"Look what I brought." Amelia holds up a head of lettuce. "We can feed Missy."

I frown. "That's not a good idea."

"Why not?"

"I used to feed Missy, but I found out doing that, or leaving a hose in the water for manatees to drink from, is bad for them. It lures them to where people and boats are, putting them in danger." I sometimes wonder if feeding Missy might be why she comes around here now, but it's been a while since I stopped and she still visits.

Amelia pouts briefly, then shrugs and returns the lettuce to her bag.

As we walk down to the dock, Deion fake-whispers, "Are we going to have to be all quiet-like now?"

Amelia bumps into him, like they've been buddies for ages. "Why? Seems like the manatees have gotten used to your annoying presence."

"Har har." Deion nudges her back.

It's true. The manatees seem to have gotten used to the three of us. Missy and Sunny swim around and sometimes one or two other manatees join them. Deion hasn't seen the dolphin yet, but I have a good feeling about it today.

We sit cross-legged on the dock, watching some boats motor by. Eventually, Missy and Sunny show up. Missy does her usual thing, nibbling at seagrasses like a large, slow vacuum cleaner. Sunny swims up to the dock where we sit, flapping his tail up and down, and pokes his stubby snout up for air.

"He's saying hi!" I say.

"I wonder what he thinks of us." Deion leans forward as far as he can without teetering into the water.

"Becca, let's see the videos you've already taken of the manatees," Amelia says. "That way we can decide what else we need to do."

My fingers tighten on my phone. I hadn't thought about how this would actually work. I'm a totally different person on my videos, and I've never shared that side of me with anyone. When I take my videos, I pretend I already have my own documentary series. I hesitate.

"Yeah, Becca, let's see 'em." Deion tilts his head to the side and gives me silly puppy eyes, practically tilting over.

Seeing both Deion and Amelia smiling and with such open expressions makes me realize they're not sitting around thinking I'm weird or a dork. They do their thing, have fun, and don't get tangled up in their thoughts like I do. I should learn from them. A warmth blossoms through me. I'm beginning to trust them. They haven't made fun of me, and they seem to love Missy and Sunny too. That goes a long way in my book.

I nod. "I'll find one." I pull up a video from a month ago, from before Missy had a baby.

The screen shows a clear shot of Missy swimming lazily near the dock. I cringe at the perkiness of my voice. "Becca Wong Walker, world-famous marine biologist, reporting. Today we're going to talk about the biology of manatees. They're marine mammals, which means they breathe air. They can hold their breath up to twenty minutes, which is a long time! Imagine that. I can only hold my breath for one minute." I pause the video, already embarrassed by my gushy reporting.

Deion looks at Amelia triumphantly. "See, even Becca's interested in how long a manatee can hold its breath."

Amelia rolls her eyes, then looks at me curiously. "You sound so different in the video."

My face warms up uncomfortably. I know I'm different when I'm by myself. If I'd known someone would watch my videos, I wouldn't have let myself loose like that. I might've used captions or nautical flags instead.

"It's great," Amelia says. "You sound so professional and knowledgeable."

"Yeah, it's pretty cool," Deion says. "Keep playing it."

When their words sink in, my lips twitch in a smile. I turn the video back on and my voice continues. "Manatees usually come up for air every five minutes. Manatee mothers and their babies will come up for air at the same time. How cute is that?"

"So cute," Amelia says. "Oh my gosh, Becca, you really are a great newscaster. We should do a series of videos about Missy and Sunny and the dolphin, with you telling people about all them and why we should care about them."

"I'd be a great newscaster too," Deion says. "Ahem." He lowers his voice. "I'm a magnifico narrator of mind-blowing science news." He snorts, barely holding back his laughter. "Listen up, *pee-awe-poe-lees*, and you will learn things you've never heard before."

A chuckle pops out of me at his inventive way of saying *peoples*.

Amelia joins in. "Right," she says, "you think people would trust a kid with a fake deep voice? Now me, on the other hand,

I can win over an audience. Watch." She flips her braids and bunches her fists on her hips in a fierce pose. "Manatee lovers, wake up! It's time to take a stand and fight the problems they face!" She turns to me. "What are the problems they face again, Becca?"

"Um." My words stumble. "A really big problem is too much development, which brings people and boats and pollution to the water. This harms the ecosystem and grasses manatees depend on."

Amelia shakes her head impatiently. "Say it like you do on the video, you know, funny and bouncy."

I blink rapidly. She sounds like Mom and Dad. *Becca bug, you shouldn't hide your wonderful personality from the world.* But hearing the words from Amelia doesn't rile me up in the same way it does when I hear it from Mom and Dad. But still, the thought of acting like myself, whatever that is, in front of others, or even now in front of Amelia and Deion, is too much.

"Look." I point to Missy and Sunny. "They're coming up for air at the same time, just like I read about."

Deion hovers over the edge of the dock, about to topple in. "So cool . . . look how their nostrils open up when they come up for air, and then close when they go down. If I had a manatee's nose, I'd beat everyone in my swim meets." He looks up. "Where's this mysterious dolphin?"

I look out over the water. "It doesn't come by every day. I've only seen it twice."

"I saw it." Amelia grins at me. "It's not just a figment of Becca's imagination. Plus, we have the video."

A surge of gratitude bubbles up. Even though Deion didn't disbelieve me, having Amelia stick up for me anyway feels great. Nobody's ever been on my side like this, even if it's for something small. I could get used to this friendship thing.

"Becca, let's go to your house and look through your videos." She links arms with mine and walk-drags me back to the house. "Earth to swimmer, you joining?"

Deion gets to his feet. "My mom's picking me up soon for swim practice. I'm bored of working on the project. Do you have an Xbox?"

We need to get to work, but I find myself saying, "We've got a Ping-Pong table."

"Ooh," Amelia says. "You've met your match. I'm a champion table tennis player."

"Really?" Deion says.

"Well, I've never actually competed in any tournaments, but I'm probably good enough," she informs us. "I win against my older brothers, and they go to college."

Deion gives her a skeptical look, and I'm with him. "You're gonna have to prove it," Deion says.

Our Ping-Pong table sits under the house. I bring out the paddles and the ball. I'm not sure how we're going to decide on the teams—supposed Ping-Pong champ versus regular players, boy versus girls, or what. I don't even know who should or how to decide these kinds of things.

"You two get over there, and I'll show you," Amelia says. Well, that takes care of that. I'm beginning to learn something hanging out with these two. Becca Wong Walker, world-famous sociologist here, observing the behavior of twelve-year-olds in the wild.

Deion and I look at each other. He shrugs and hands me the extra paddle. "You're gonna regret it," he says to Amelia.

I'm pretty good at Ping-Pong—not amazing, but I have a mean backhand that's unstoppable about a third of the time. This is probably where I should jump in and talk trash too. But I don't.

"Let's spell *manatee* to see who starts." Amelia bounces the ball to our side, and I return it. "M . . ."

She hits it. "A . . ."

Deion bats it. "N . . ."

She slams a vicious one on us and yells, "A!"

It whooshes by between Deion and me. Under normal rules, after spelling P-I-N-G, we would start the game, but Deion says, "Let's do it again, until we spell the whole word."

We try again and get to M-A-N-A-T, then M-A-N, then M-A-N-A-T-E. Amelia has a mad grin on her face.

"Come on, are y'all even trying?" Deion says.

We've forgotten to be competitive and we're trying to keep the ball going.

"M . . ." Bounce. "A . . ." Hit. "N . . ." Bounce. "A . . ." We chant in unison, my voice blending in under Amelia's and Deion's increasingly loud shouts. "T . . . E . . . E!"

Amelia collapses across the table with a laugh, and Deion raises his arms in victory.

A thrill runs through me. I can't believe I have not one but two actual friends. I laugh and say, "Let's do that again."

9

After Deion's mom picks him up, I take Amelia to my room. It's been a long time since someone besides my family has been here. I wish I'd known she was coming up, because I would've cleaned it up. She's going to think I'm a big slob with my clothes all over the place. When we get to the room, Amelia doesn't seem to notice. She peers at the many manatee photos pinned to my bulletin board. "You're not kidding about loving manatees," she says. "Oh, this one is sooo cute."

I look away, caught between embarrassment and hope. She said it in a nice way, not like she was making fun of me, but I'm not used to this kind of attention. Hearing her excitement lifts me up. She and I are more alike than I thought—we both squeal over cute manatee pics. In the safety of my room, and with only Amelia around, things feel looser, easier.

"Why do you think that dolphin is up here in the river?" Amelia asks.

I've been thinking about this puzzle. "I was reading dolphins will go up into rivers to find food."

"I wonder if fresh water is bad for them," Amelia muses.

"A while ago, a bunch of people made a human chain to herd some dolphins that got stuck in a channel up in St. Petersburg." Talking about dolphins with Amelia feels comfortable, almost easy.

"Really? How cool." She plops down at my desk. "Let's see some more of your videos."

I'm not sure I want her to see more of my hyped-up videos. She was nice about it at the dock, but that was probably because she only got a little dose of the real me. "How about we go back out to the river and make new ones?" I say.

"Okay. I have some time before I need to go in for dinner."

"What about Deion? Should we wait for him?"

She twists her lips. "Nah. He's not taking this seriously. We'll catch him up at school."

I feel bad excluding Deion, but it makes sense. Amelia and I live next door to each other, where the manatees are. We can't stop scientific research when he's not around. We're on manatee time, not Deion time.

Back at the river, I pull out my phone and start panning. Everything is calm. No manatees or dolphins in sight.

The drone of a boat engine overpowers the quiet. *RRRRRRRMMM.* A flat-bottomed boat zips by, creating twin trails of white wake behind it.

"Hey!" Amelia leaps to her feet and waves her arms wildly. "Slow down!" I can't believe she's yelling at these hostile-looking guys, with their crab pots, camouflage vests, and dead-eyed stares.

No sooner than the boat has gone by, a couple of people on Jet Skis carom by. "Minimum wake zone!" she yells at them. One of the riders, a guy in his twenties maybe, glances briefly at us as he zooms by.

I leap to my feet too. "There are manatees here," I say in a voice no one hears. Tears prick my eyes. It's not fair the manatees are at the mercy of boats and Jet Skis. And even now, I can't raise my voice.

"Oh, jeez," Amelia says. "What are we going to do about this? Did you record them? We should report them."

I look down and my heart sinks. When the boat and Jet Skis barreled their way through, I was so upset I didn't pay attention to my phone. All I have is shaky video of my feet and the dock and the sound of Amelia yelling at the boaters.

I had one job, and I messed it up. My face warms again, and my insides squinch together. But this time, instead of wishing I could fall through the dock or run away, a hot anger flares in me. Missy and Sunny deserve better.

"Come on."

"Where are we going?"

I lead Amelia back up to Mom's studio, where I've finished painting the signs. "We have to do something. Help me put these up."

Amelia's face lights up when she sees the large signs leaning against a wall. Instead of my original angry ideas, I ended up with two signs where I painted Missy and Sunny swimming happily. One reads, MOVE LIKE A MANATEE, WITH MINIMUM WAKE, and the other says, MAKE A MAXIMUM DIFFERENCE FOR MANATEES: MINIMUM WAKE, PLEASE.

"So cool! How are we going to put them up?"

I show her some wire stakes Mom got. "We'll use these."

We take the signs and stakes back down to the riverbank. I show her how to fit the stakes into the corrugated plastic signs, and then it's a matter of finding the right place for them.

Pushing the signs into the ground makes me feel better. But it's not enough. Thinking of that smug guy on a Jet Ski is enraging. "Amelia, can we ask your dad to take us up the river?"

She stares at me. "What does my dad have to do with anything? You want to go after those jet skiers?"

"No, of course not." I definitely wouldn't confront strangers. "There are so many more boats headed upriver recently. I want to know why. Your dad is renovating some houses, and there could be other construction or something."

Amelia furrows her brow. "I care about the manatees, I do, but I don't want to mess with my parents' business. Let's just record videos for our science project and leave my dad out of it."

My heart hammers and my breath grows shallow. I said what I wanted to, and Amelia shut me down. This is why I don't speak up—what if I angered Amelia just as we're becoming friends? Now I might lose my only new friend. Maybe she's right—we should stick to the plan of making a PSA. We can still help Missy and Sunny by warning boaters about speeding.

She looks at me like she's waiting for me to say something.

Now that I think about it, her tone of voice wasn't mean. She didn't make fun of me. She looks annoyed, but not at me. I push myself to speak up again. "Can you ask him anyway? I'd like to see his Airbnbs."

Amelia's mouth turns down. "I'll see what kind of mood he's in tonight, and maybe I'll ask him."

My heart is still doing its palpitations, but it's calming down. "Thanks."

What do you know. I didn't sink through the floor or faint, and Amelia didn't mock me. I'll take that small victory.

Later, Amelia texts me. *My dad will take us on his boat tomorrow after school.*

Awesome. Let's ask Deion to join us too.

Okay. Later, gator.

I put down the phone, flop back on my bed, and let out a relieved sigh. It's a small thing, but I pushed back and nothing terrible happened. Amelia is still my friend. Now I just have to worry about what to say to her dad about his Airbnbs.

10

Amelia, Deion, and I sit in her dad's motorboat. She's made sure her dad knows we're in a minimum wake zone, so we putter slowly up the calm, wide water. A warm breeze flutters my hair, and birdcalls drift through the air.

"I'm glad you're interested in seeing the houses we're working on." Mr. Carlson wears a Tampa Bay Rays cap and mirrored sunglasses, his tanned, leathery hands resting on the boat's wheel. "You said it was for a school project? About what—construction and development?"

I look at Amelia, who shrugs. I wonder what she told her dad to get him to take us on this trip.

"Um, not exactly. We're doing some research on manatees," Amelia says.

"What do manatees have to do with my houses?"

Amelia looks to me, but I shake my head, like, *Don't make me talk to your dad.* She juts her chin out, like, *You're the one who wanted to do this.* I feel my mouth go dry. "I've noticed a lot more boats coming up this way," I say. "They're a danger to the manatees in the river."

Mr. Carlson glances over at me. "Huh."

Deion chimes in. "We want to take a look around, you know, to see how many boats and docks there are. It's like a statistics thing." I don't really know what statistics are, but I don't think Deion does either.

"That's nice," Mr. Carlson says, distracted. He doesn't seem to understand why we want to see his Airbnbs, but that's okay. "We're renovating a couple of the houses, and the other one has renters in it now. We're almost there."

Riding on the water is always mesmerizing. I love the gentle up-and-down motion, the water slipping by, and the trees rolling along the bank. It's even more fun on a kayak with Grandma, when we're up close to the overhanging branches and competing to identify the herons, hawks, woodpeckers, and other birds. I envy the manatees and dolphins that get to live and play in the water all the time.

We arrive at the dock of a large white house on stilts with a covered porch. The lawn leading up to it is perfectly green and flat, with small, bushy palm trees marking the border of the property. Next to it is a similar house and lawn. They look fancy and very different from the more down-to-earth houses along the rest of the river.

"Whoa. Those are some houses," Deion says.

"We're proud of what we're doing," Mr. Carlson says. "We have a couple other ones farther upstream." He gestures to the house next door, where two Jet Skis are tied to the dock. "Vacation renters are in that one while we're getting ready to put this one on the market."

Amelia and I exchange glances. Those might be the Jet Skis we saw yesterday.

When we arrive, Mr. Carlson ties up the boat and we step onto the dock. We approach the house and go under the stilts to a set of stairs that leads up. The door is open and we hear voices inside.

"Your moms are here," Mr. Carlson says. "Marcie and Allison, I brought the girls over. This is their friend Deion."

Deion gives them a half wave.

"Hello, kids." Mom stands with Amelia's mom in the kitchen. They're looking over fabric swatches and photos on the kitchen island. "I'm helping Marcie figure out color schemes for this house. I have some great pieces that could go in the family room."

I'm not surprised to see them together, because Mom's been talking about her new friend Marcie ever since they moved in. But I'm a bit surprised to see her here. Mom's thing is more wicker baskets and rag rugs, not this contemporary and sleek stuff.

Mrs. Carlson grins. "Your mom is helping me stage these homes to help sell them. We're going for a casual and eclectic Florida vibe, and your mom's art and furniture is perfect. People love this look."

I smile blankly. Designer talk usually goes in one ear and out the other. I'd much prefer to think about marine biology or manatees, though the thought of how Jet Skis could run over manatees sours my mood. Worse is the sinking feeling that my own mom and Amelia's parents are on the wrong side of this equation. More Airbnbs will bring more boats and Jet Skis. Last night I worried about pushing Amelia away, but now my mom is involved too.

I can't hold it in anymore. "What about the Jet Skis?"

Mom looks puzzled. "What do you mean?"

"The guys who are renting the house next door were on their Jet Skis. They were zooming around, not paying attention to the minimum wake signs."

"They were very disconsiderate," Deion says.

"Inconsiderate," I say in a low voice.

"Inconsiderate," he says, as if that's what he meant all along.

Amelia says hesitantly, "Dad, can you talk to them about it?"

Her dad gives her a sharp look. "All the rules are in our rental packet." He gestures to a folder that no one probably ever reads. "My guests don't need to be pestered about environmental issues when they just want to relax."

Amelia's mom looks up. "It might not be a bad idea to let them know they're breaking the law when they create more than a minimal wake."

Mr. Carlson shakes his head impatiently. "No need to rile them up. It's never good business to antagonize paying guests."

Amelia looks from one of her parents to the other and rushes out to the covered patio overlooking the water.

Deion and I follow.

"Let's go talk to those guys anyway," Deion says.

Amelia shakes her head. "I changed my mind. If we make the guests mad, they'll leave bad reviews and that'll just make my parents fight more." She pushes past us. "I'm going outside."

Deion and I look at each other. After a moment, we follow her. When we get down the stairs, Amelia has run ahead to the river's edge, where she crouches, fascinated by something by the water.

I'm stumped. Videos and signs are fine, but I need to be able to fight for Missy and Sunny in person too. What kind of manatee protector am I if I can't even talk to a couple of guys next door?

Deion must be feeling the same thing, because he turns to me. "Let's go talk to them. We don't need anyone's permission."

His determined expression steadies me. I glance over to the house next door and see two guys swinging in hammocks under the house.

I blink. "Okay, let's do it."

11

I'm not sure how we're going to just casually walk over next door to talk to the guys. I notice a box by the staircase with some balls and a Frisbee. That's it. I pick up the Frisbee. "Deion, let's play with this and throw it into the next yard."

He laughs. "Got it." He grabs the Frisbee and runs out to the lawn. "Catch!" He slings it my way.

I catch it and fling the Frisbee back. My back's to the yard next door, near the palm trees. Deion takes aim and whizzes the Frisbee past my head and between two palms, landing it in the next yard. "My bad," he calls out loudly. "Sorry I threw the Frisbee too hard, and it landed in the next yard!"

I muffle a laugh at his over-the-top act, but I gotta hand it to him, it's what we set out to do.

We walk over next door and come to the two guys in the

hammocks. One of them is holding a beer, and the other is swinging with one leg hanging out, earbuds in, eyes half closed.

Deion heads over to the Frisbee and calls out, "Don't mind us. Just picking up our Frisbee that came over completely accidentally."

"Yo," the one with the beer calls out lazily. He and the other guy look to be in their twenties, though I can't tell for sure because adults look pretty much the same to me.

Deion raises a brow at me and mutters under his breath, "Are you going to say something?"

"Um . . ." I give him my *What? Are you kidding? I'm not talking to these guys* face, even though they seem pretty chill and it's hard to imagine these are the same don't-care-about-manatees speed freaks we saw yesterday. Still. Thinking about confronting them is very different from actually doing it. Plus, it's hard to go against my no-talking-to-strangers rule, which has served me well all my life.

Deion walks over. "Are those your Jet Skis?"

The guy with the beer looks at him. "Nah. We're on vacation. They came with the house."

Deion nudges me.

The universe is conspiring against me. Or testing me. Or both.

One of the guys takes a swig of his beer. He looks at me impassively. It's not a mean look, but it's not friendly either.

I gulp and look down. Nothing comes out of my mouth. I know I'm letting down Missy and Sunny, all their manatee friends, and their new dolphin buddy, but I can't do it. I can't speak up. Again.

"My friend saw your Jet Skis yesterday," Deion says. "It's a minimum wake manatee zone, so you gotta slow down so you don't leave a huge wake."

I'm flooded with relief and dismay that Deion had to say what I couldn't.

The guy snorts. "What're we supposed to do? The point of Jet Skis is to go fast."

His friend looks over. "There are manatees here? Cool."

I blink rapidly, still tongue-tied.

"Yo, man. Go farther out to the bay to jet ski," Deion says, "or try a kayak."

"It's not going to make a difference if we stop," the guy with the earbuds says. "There are other boats and Jet Skis on the water."

I want to tell him every person makes a difference and if they did their part, they'd make a small dent in the problem, but my heart thuds and I say nothing, even when it's Missy's and Sunny's lives at stake. I kick myself inwardly at how useless I am.

"Think about it." Deion raises the Frisbee in a wave.

The guy shrugs and finishes his beer. He crushes the can and tosses it on the ground.

I open my mouth like a fish, and Deion and I walk away, back to the other property. What is wrong with me? My face burns as I hurry past the palms.

As we get out of earshot, I mutter to Deion, "Thanks for helping out."

He looks at me curiously. "S'okay." He brightens. "Those guys said they'd think about slowing down."

I'm dubious. I don't remember them saying anything that sounded promising.

Amelia watches us approach. "Why'd you do that? I asked you not to talk to them." Her face twitches, like she's about to cry. "You're going to ruin things for my parents. Some friends you are." She turns and storms back to the house.

My heart sinks.

Deion gives me a puzzled look. "What's up with her?" He smiles and tosses the Frisbee into the air. "That was cool. We're like the Manatee Vigilantes. No, that doesn't sound right. We're the Manatee Marauders." It's like he doesn't even care that he upset her. He's making jokes, again.

I shake my head and push past him. "Not now." Those guys didn't promise anything, and I was no help. Not only did we basically fail, but I still got Amelia mad at me. She's right. Those guys will probably complain and her parents will fight more and she'll never talk to me again and it wasn't worth it because we didn't even help the manatees. I'm so frustrated with myself, and to make things worse, I don't know how to make things better with Amelia. But I know I need to try.

Inside, Amelia sits on a brown leather couch in the open, bright living room. She's on her phone, her face stony.

I sit down next to her. She is liking some random kid's

pictures, ignoring me. I know she knows I'm right here, because she shifts slightly away.

"I'm sorry," I say. "I didn't mean to make you mad."

"It's fine. I'm not mad," she says without looking up. Everything about her expression and posture says that's a lie. She puts down her phone. "We're supposed to be working on a manatee education video, not ruining my life!"

I flinch. "What do you mean?"

"If this Airbnb thing doesn't work out and my parents lose money, we'll have to move again." Tears prick at her eyes. "I hate it when they fight over money."

This is terrible. The first time I tried to help Missy and Sunny in a concrete way may be the reason I lose my first real friend. "I don't know what to say."

"You never know what to say," she spits out.

Her words strike me like jagged rocks.

Her eyes flare wide, like she surprised herself too, but she quickly goes back to her phone, tapping away.

I push myself up and find Mom in the kitchen. "Can you take me home?" I try to keep the thickness out of my voice.

Mom gives me her *super-worried* look and glances at

Mrs. Carlson. "Sure. Marcie, let's finish this later. Does Deion need a ride too?"

I glance out the window to the lawn, where Deion is tossing the Frisbee into the air and giving it enough spin for it to return to him. He still seems happy as ever, as if nothing has happened. I don't want to deal with his jokes right now, so I shake my head a little at my mom to let her know I want to be alone.

"It's fine, we'll get him home," Mrs. Carlson says brightly, her eyes darting between Amelia and me on the couch.

We head out. What a disaster. I failed Missy and Sunny, *and* Amelia hates me.

12

When we get home, I head straight to the backyard, my happy place by the river. All I want now is to see Missy and Sunny and forget about Amelia's cutting words. I'm sure seeing them slip through the water, chewing on seagrass, Sunny nuzzling at his mom's side, will calm me down.

I clomp down the dock, dangle my legs off the end, and let out a heavy sigh. The breeze sends ripples of water lapping against the dock. "Missy and Sunny, wherever you are, I wish you could help," I say into the water, as if they were here. "I thought I was brave enough to confront those tourists, but it made Amelia angry and scared her parents will lose their business. And even my parents want more tourists to come." On the ride home, Mom went on and on about how much fun it'd be to work on the new Airbnbs, probably trying to cheer me up, but all she did was remind me she's part of the problem too.

Out on the water, circular ripples make their way toward me. Missy and Sunny are back!

I scramble to my feet.

"Missy, Sunny, you're here." Seeing their cute faces coming over immediately lifts my spirits.

Missy swims over to me, and Sunny follows. He's getting to be such a great swimmer. I kneel down and hold out my arm in a greeting. I don't have any food to offer them, but Missy seems curious and comes closer. Sunny hangs back.

"Oh, Sunny, don't be afraid of me." I wiggle my fingers.

Sunny tucks himself close to his mom.

I take out my camera. It's time to take some footage that could be useful for our video project. "It's another seventy-degree day in sunny Florida. Missy and Sunny are here, but we're on dolphin watch. According to my research, it's very rare to see dolphins and manatees hanging around together."

Missy and Sunny are on the move today, and they glide away, flapping their tails. I keep the video trained on their ripples as they move to the center of the river.

The distinctive dorsal fin of a dolphin slices by right near them. "The dolphin is back. They really are friends!" I say.

My camera follows their progress. I can see Missy and Sunny, a large and a small shape moving along the bottom of the river. The dolphin zooms past the manatees and toward me. It comes almost to the dock, turns its head and looks at me with one eye, then swims back to where Missy and Sunny are. I bite my lip so I don't squeal. I've never seen a dolphin so close. Its smiling face is so friendly!

It's obviously much quicker than Missy and Sunny. It circles them, its fin showing up and coming back. It seems curious and frisky, like it wants to play with them. I can just imagine Missy pushing Sunny out of the way, her maternal instincts kicking in. I want to let her know, don't worry, the dolphin just wants to play.

I keep the video on, staying quiet to not disturb this magical scene—splashing dolphin, milling manatees, and birdsong in the air.

But then—*VRRROOOOMMMM*.

The horrifying sound of a motorboat approaching. I turn the camera toward the sound and capture a boat speeding right toward Missy and Sunny! Time seems to slow as a man in a baseball cap and sunglasses sits at the wheel and a woman lounges on the seat behind, a floppy hat half-covering her face.

My heart is caught in my throat, and I'm stuck to the dock. My voice dries out and I can't speak. This is my worst nightmare and I'm about to watch it happen. There's no way the manatees can get away in time.

The boat bears down on the spot where I last saw Sunny's little circular footprint.

With a flash, the dolphin swims between the manatees and the boat and leaps fully out of the water into the air, blocking the path of the boat. Its skin glistens and drops of water spray in a glistening arc.

The boat veers in a sharp turn, narrowly avoiding hitting the dolphin and Missy and Sunny. Shouts from the passengers carry across the water.

"Did you see that?"

"A dolphin!"

The dolphin squeaks and whistles and swims away. Missy and Sunny move along, not noticing the whole commotion.

I keep recording the boat, which has slowed down. A woman leans out the back, pointing and yelling. The boat turns around to follow the dolphin, which has swum away, sleek and fast.

"The dolphin saved their lives," I say into the video. "I just witnessed the most incredible thing. The dolphin that's been hanging around this river put itself in front of a speeding boat about to hit the manatees and jumped into the air. It risked its own life to save its friends."

I turn off the video, my hands shaking. I just got video evidence of an incredible manatee rescue.

13

I run into the house, but Mom is on a conference call, and Dad's still at work.

I want to text Amelia, but my stomach clenches as I remember she's mad at me about the jet skiers and I'm mad at her for telling me I never have anything to say.

But she would want to know about the dolphin. I really want to share this with her. Is this what it means to have a friend? It's awful how for a brief moment it seemed like we were real friends, and now I've lost her. Maybe I should try to reach out. I know she'll love this video.

I can't hold it inside anymore. I text her, *The most amazing thing just happened.*

An interminable row of dots blinks on my screen. I squirm,

wondering what she's typing. Maybe she's telling me to leave her alone.

Finally, she writes back. *What?*

Can you come over? I'll show you.

A long pause. *Let me ask my mom.*

An even longer pause. *I'll be over.*

I pace around my room, almost bouncing off the walls. I watch the video again—*the dolphin leaps into the air*, and then again—*the boat veers away from the manatees.* My delighted laughter escapes with each amazing moment. The video is looping for the third time when the doorbell rings.

I run to the door and fling it open. Amelia has a cautious expression, like she's not sure whether I'm still mad at her or she's still mad at me. The thrill of seeing the dolphin save Missy and her baby buzzes through me.

"Come in." I pull her toward my bedroom.

Amelia's eyes widen. "What's with the huge smile?" she says with a tentative grin.

I must look weird, but I don't care anymore. People outside my family never see my I-don't-care-what-people-think-of-me personality. "I just saw an amazing sight on the river and got it on video."

We get to my room and plop on my bed. I hand over my phone. "Watch this."

She sits on my bed cautiously and takes the phone. The video plays the scene I've already come to memorize. Missy and Sunny swim with their tails, making the circular ripples on the water's surface, the dolphin's fin appears and disappears, the boat zooms into view, the dolphin leaps into the air, and the boat turns sharply away.

Amelia's face transforms as she watches. "Ohmigosh!" she squeals. "Did that dolphin just save Missy and Sunny from being hit?"

"Yes."

"You caught it so perfectly. It's like a movie."

Her words give me an idea. "This video would be perfect for our PSA on the dangers of boating."

Amelia stares at me and claps her hands. "You're right. The video's super dramatic, so people will have to pay attention. And we can talk about the dolphins and manatees being friends. How cute is that? I love stories of odd animal friendships."

A smile spreads across my face.

"This is much better than yelling at my parents' Airbnb guests," Amelia says.

My smile slips. I was hoping she was over that.

She stares at her hands, wringing them. A frown flickers across her face. "I'm sorry for what I said back at the Airbnb." She sighs. "I hate it when my parents fight, and the thing they fight most about is their business. Even so, it was a mean thing to say."

A huge weight lifts from my chest. "I'm sorry too," I say. "Deion and I should've talked to you before going off to confront those guys."

Amelia gives me a wavery smile.

"Let's tell Deion about this video," I say.

"I'll call him." Amelia texts him, and pretty soon, he's on the screen.

"What's up?" Deion is walking around his backyard. He plops down on a lawn chair.

"You've got to see this video that Becca took of the dolphin and Missy and Sunny," Amelia says.

"What? You were there without me?" Deion's brows beetle together. "We're supposed to be a team."

Amelia and I exchange looks. I just managed to get back on Amelia's good side and now Deion's mad at me? This is why I haven't had friends before. It's way too complicated. I didn't even think he cared. He acts like nothing bothers him. I try to see if he's messing with us, but no, he actually seems upset.

Amelia stares intently at him. "Dude," she says. "We totally did think of you. We're calling you right now, aren't we? You can't be here with us all the time. We live here. You don't."

Amelia always knows what to say. I add, "Don't be mad. You should see this video. It's really good."

Deion's face softens. A small thrill goes through me. Something I said changed his mood.

"So the dolphin actually exists? You have proof?" Deion says.

"Oh, better than proof. It'll blow your mind." Amelia turns to me. "Send him the video?"

"Hold on." I text Deion the video.

While we wait for him to watch it, Amelia air drums her knees and sings off-key, "Oh manatees, oh manatees, how much we love thees. You are the best cows of the world, because you are the cows of the seas . . ."

I burst into giggles and join her. She sing-shouts while I

softly harmonize, "Oh manatees, oh manatees, how much we love thees."

Deion comes back to the screen. "That was amazing. What're we going to do with it?"

"We were thinking we could make this the main part of our science project." I explain what Amelia and I talked about.

"Let's do it," Deion says. "The Manatee Marauders are on the case!"

Amelia snorts. "Okay. Let's make this PSA the place where we reveal the footage. It will be amazing to surprise everyone with this dolphin playing with manatees."

"Yeah." Deion breaks into a grin. "If this is one of the first times a dolphin has saved manatees, it's also something scientists could study. Our science project could make a difference."

I nod, liking this new Deion, who actually cares. It sounds like we have a plan. Hearing my friends talk about the PSA as something that might actually change people's minds fills me with both anticipation and a little dread.

After Amelia leaves, Mom and Dad come home. I can't wait to show them the video of the dolphin and manatee, so I herd them into our family room as soon as they've taken off their shoes.

"That's extraordinary," Mom says after they've watched it. "What are you going to do with it?"

"We're going to use it to make a PSA about the dangers of boats to manatees for our science project."

"That's great," Dad says. "While you work on that, I need to do some work before dinner. The boating sports festival is on the city council agenda in a couple of weeks, and I have to work on some figures," Dad says.

"What are they voting on?" Mom asks.

"Whether to go ahead with our proposal. We're going to need to go through some environmental reviews for the temporary moorings that'll be installed for the demos and races. I'll be presenting the economic case for the festival."

I look up. "Temporary moorings?"

"Yes, the city will need to create places for all the boats to tie up."

This boat-a-palooza or whatever Dad's calling his X Games of boats is a terrible idea. "Dad," I say, "all those boats are going to be dangerous for the manatees."

Dad gives me a thoughtful look. "Lots of boats and tourists already go visit the manatees during the winter. They seem to be doing fine. Weren't manatees declared no longer endangered recently?"

This is something I know about. "They're threatened, which is less protection, but most of the scientists who studied manatees were against the change."

Mom leans in. "That's interesting. How do you know that?"

"I've been reading about manatees for the past two years."

"I'm sure the manatees will be fine," Dad says. "The city will go through an environmental review and make sure the festival pays attention to the manatees."

Mom says, "Becca, your video is really something else. You should show it to your teacher."

"You're changing the subject," I say. Mom is doing that thing she does, where she doesn't disagree with Dad outright, but if she doesn't agree, she'll try to ignore their differences. I guess it's better than the way Amelia's parents fight.

Mom gives me a crooked smile. "Maybe, but I'm still right. Talk to Ms. Amato."

“When did you say the city council is meeting?” I ask Dad.

“In a couple of weeks.”

A prick of unease nags at me. In two weeks, the city council could approve Dad’s plan for Boat Olympics. It’s going to be held in the bay, which isn’t in the minimum wake zone, but manatees hang out there too. Somebody’s got to speak up for Missy and Sunny, but I’m not brave enough. And even if I were, how could I go against Dad and his business?

I head to my room, racking my brain for a way to make a difference and help Missy and Sunny and their manatee friends.

14

Amelia, Deion, and I lean over the railing of the walkway at the wildlife sanctuary. In the tank below us, two fat manatees slowly swim around.

I spend Sunday afternoons with Grandma whenever Mom drags Dad to flea markets, so I convinced her to bring us here, figuring we could get more background info on manatees. Plus, it'll be nice to spend time with my new friends. It's a nature reserve that helps animals that've been hurt. They have a Florida panther; a gray fox; a lot of birds, like a one-legged hawk and a bald eagle with a broken wing; a reptile hut with snakes and lizards; and a bunch of other animals. When I was smaller, I loved playing with the touch tank, but now it feels sad. I know these animals can't survive in the wild and are safe here, but I can't help comparing them with their cousins that are free.

"This manatee is Gertrude and the other is Parker," the park lady says.

"Why're they here?" Amelia leans against the railing, wiggling her fingers at the manatees.

"Gertrude was rescued a year ago. She was hit by a boat and had severe internal injuries. Now she has problems with buoyancy. She can't go back to the wild, because she can't sink to the bottom to eat the seagrasses."

The big fat manatee moves slowly back and forth in a large tank. *Gertrude,* I think, *do you have a baby somewhere out in the world?* "What about Parker?"

"Parker was born in captivity, so she wouldn't survive in the wild. She wouldn't know how to feed off the eelgrass or where to go when the weather gets cold. Manatees are like elephants—they rely on their memories to go back to the warm springs each winter, and it's their mothers who teach them that. A manatee born in captivity doesn't have that knowledge."

The woman feeds the manatees head after head of romaine lettuce. She takes them out of a huge carton and tosses sixteen heads of lettuce to each. "These girls are on a diet because they don't swim enough to keep their weight down. We feed them eighty pounds of lettuce a day. In the wild, manatees eat ten percent of their body weight a day, which can be a hundred and fifty or two hundred pounds of seagrass," the woman explains.

"That's a lot of farting," Deion says.

Amelia and I giggle. I imagine bubbles of fart trailing behind the manatees.

"You're right." She smiles. "In fact, manatees control their buoyancy with their farts."

We all laugh.

"I wonder if it propels them forward," Deion says. "That would come in handy in a swim meet—Deion, the Mean, Lean Farting Machine." He raises his arms and lets out a crowd-roar noise.

The park ranger hides her smile and continues. "In the wild, manatees are an important part of the food chain. They're like lawn mowers, eating the older parts of the seagrass and keeping them healthy. If they didn't eat the seagrass, the grass would grow so quickly and thickly, boats and fish couldn't get through the shallow waters. They also spread seeds through their poop and stir up the baby fish and shrimp hiding in the grass when they eat. This allows bigger fish to eat the little fish, and eventually the apex predators eat those fish."

"Manatee poop makes the world go round." Deion snickers.

"Pretty much."

"It's the circle of life," Amelia says.

Now my sides hurt from laughing. But I can't help feeling sad for these manatees who'll never get to swim free and far, roaming the Gulf of Mexico or the Atlantic Ocean.

As we leave, a college-aged girl sits at a table with some flyers by the parking lot. "Will you sign a petition to stop the toll road?" she calls out.

Grandma walks over with a bright, interested expression, and I follow. Amelia bounds up next to me and Deion saunters over too.

"Hey there." She hands me a flyer with a picture of a scared-looking manatee and some bullet points. "The state legislature recently approved a toll road that will come through this community. It will break up the estuary and spring ecosystem that manatees, birds, and other wildlife depend on, and it'll bring a lot of development to the area."

I wrinkle my brows. Dad was talking about this at the barbecue the other day. "Is it a done deal? Can people stop it?" I pick up the girl's flyer and run my finger across the logo, three interlocking Cs, for Citizens Concerned about the Connectors.

"Good question," she says. "There are several task force meetings studying the roads where people can provide comments. The more people we can get to sign this petition showing they're against it, the better."

"I'll sign it," Deion says.

"Sorry, you have to be over eighteen."

"Who says I'm not over eighteen," Deion says in his fake deep voice.

Grandma's reading the flyer carefully.

"Are you going to sign it?" I ask.

"Yes, of course. This is unconscionable." She takes the offered pen and signs her name. "Did you know I was a teen on the first Earth Day in 1970? My friends and I skipped school to go pick up trash by the river." The girl smiles, and they chat about environmental activism, past and present.

Somehow Grandma signing the petition feels both like a big deal and like nothing. I let out a deep breath as we walk to the truck.

It's not fair. Missy and Sunny can't catch a break. They just want to live their own lives, nibbling seagrass and playing in the water. They want to stay warm in the winter and swim far and wide in the summer. But everywhere they go, they face dangers—from boats and algae and fishing lines—and now they could lose their homes when the toll road cuts through the land and brings in even more people, cars, and condos.

Even more horribly, Amelia's and my parents are all part of the forces that could harm Missy and Sunny. Dad's bringing the festival of boats and Mom's helping the Carlsons with their fancy Airbnbs. Having our parents on the wrong side of the manatees is a horrible feeling. Why don't the people I love care about the manatees as much as I do?

I'm so frustrated. I'm mad at them, but I'm mostly mad at myself. No matter how much I promise to help Missy and Sunny, I haven't figured out a way to actually make a difference.

I lag behind as the others walk to the truck. I stare at the video I took of the dolphin saving Missy and Sunny. This dolphin didn't think and agonize over what to do. It used its instincts to protect other living creatures. It just did it.

Well, so can I. My heart pounds and my hands shake.

I glance at Amelia and Deion. They wanted to wait to use the video in the PSA, but I don't think we can wait. Missy, Sunny, and the dolphin need help now.

I look at the little lock symbol on the video showing it's private, only viewable by me. After a moment, I type a title and a few sentences under the video:

Amazing Manatee Rescue by Dolphin

Near the Two Brothers Springs, a dolphin risks its own life to save a group of manatees from a speeding boat. Boats are one of the main reasons manatees are killed each year. Don't be the boat. Be the dolphin!

If I make this video public, I can send it to the city council to make them see the danger of the boating festival, and they'll have to change their plans. I can't think about how mad at me Dad might get for going against him. For a moment, I feel bad. I promised Deion not to leave him out anymore. And Amelia will probably feel betrayed—the boating festival would be good for her parents' business too.

But I can't just keep doing nothing. Missy and Sunny got lucky once. It might not happen again.

I take a breath and set it to public.

Let people see what a dolphin can do. Let it lead the way.

15

We're in the truck, pulling out of the parking lot. After a few moments, my phone dings to let me know there was a view and a like on the video. A small thrill runs through me. Aside from Mom, Dad, Amelia, Deion, and Grandma, no one else knows about or has ever seen my videos.

Now someone out there—I don't know who—has watched the video and liked it. I don't know how they even found it already—I haven't had a chance to look up the city council members to send it to them.

Gulp. Maybe I'll take a break and pass out. Someone I don't know has watched the video.

Another ding, and another. Each ding makes my heart beat a little faster and my face grow warmer. I'm not even on the video, but I feel like I'm on display. A gray dread blooms like a mushroom inside me. I made the video public so people at the city council could see it, but I didn't expect anybody else to watch it.

Grandma glances at me. "What's that?"

I hastily turn off the notifications. "Um, nothing."

"Who wants some frozen yogurt?" she asks.

"Me," Amelia, Deion, and I all say at the same time.

"Jinx," Amelia says.

"Nah, who does jinx anymore," Deion says.

"Are you rejecting the power of jinx?" Amelia says.

"That's right. I reject it completely."

I need the power of something to keep my mind off the video.

Grandma drives us to the Froyo Emporium. There were so many of these a few years ago, but this one's the only one left in town, the last stubborn holdout of the frozen yogurt fad. I mean, it's delicious, it's a great idea, so why shouldn't it stick to its confetti-colored dreams?

I glance down at my phone, and my heart does a triple flip. The likes are cycling up, *blip*, *blip*, *blip*. It's only been a few minutes, and the video already has 135 views. At this rate, I need to let Amelia and Deion know I made the video public.

"Look." I show my phone to them in the back seat.

"Whoa," Deion says. "That your video?"

I nod. My face feels like I've been out too long on a hot summer day.

Amelia frowns. "Why'd you publish it without talking to us about it? We agreed to wait until our science project to use it."

A tight feeling squeezes me, like I can't breathe. She's right. I knew Amelia and Deion didn't want to share the video right away, and I ignored their wishes.

Deion leans in, sticking his nose almost to the screen. "You're cooking."

My heart does its pitter-pat workout. "I . . . I'm sorry I didn't talk to you about it. I couldn't stand the idea of Missy and Sunny being in danger one minute more. I thought if I posted it, we could change the city council's mind."

Amelia sags and looks out the car window.

"It's going wild, up to two hundred views!" Deion punches the air. "I'm going to share this." He digs out his phone.

"Wait," I say. "Amelia, we can still do our project. This will help us get attention for it."

"This is the second time you did something without thinking about what I want," Amelia says.

This hits me in the gut. Am I a terrible, selfish person? I'm not used to thinking about what my friends might want when I've never had friends before.

"What's this video?" Grandma asks.

"Remember the video I showed you of the dolphin saving Missy and Sunny?" It was the first thing I did when she came to pick me up today.

"Of course. It was so interesting."

"I just made it public, and lots of people are liking it now." I glance at Amelia and sigh. "It's a good thing."

Amelia's expression changes from a glower to a more neutral look. "Okay," she says. "I *don't* like secrets, but you're right. We need to spread the word to stop boats from hitting manatees." She pulls out her phone. "Liking and sharing."

I lean my head against the headrest and close my eyes. After this roller coaster of emotions, frozen yogurt will hit the spot.

We arrive at the Froyo store and make our way in. I'm temporarily distracted by the yumminess all around. I get my usual chocolate base and add my favorite toppings: gummy bears, strawberries, and chocolate chips.

"How does that site work?" Grandma asks. "Are you safe online?"

"Yes, it doesn't identify me or anything. My name on the account is Ms. Manatee." One of the reasons I was even able to post the video was because only my voice is identifiable. I don't show my face or name anywhere.

I put away my phone. "I don't want to think about it now." I dig into my treat. If there's one thing I'm very serious about—aside from manatees—it's enjoying every bite of my frozen yogurt. I don't want any distractions from the creamy smooth taste of chocolate with the crunch of chocolate chips and chewy goodness of gummy bears.

Deion nods emphatically. "Yeah, man. This is much too good to not pay our hundred percent full attention to. Mmmm-mmmh." After a few minutes, he looks up. "What's the number of likes on that video now?"

I wake up my phone.

The view count is at 579, and the numbers are switching even faster than before.

Amelia looks at me with wide eyes. "Becca, your video is going viral."

16

Amelia was right.

It wasn't quite viral when I went to sleep—1,200 views—but when I woke up this morning and turned on my phone, it had exploded to over 28,000 views, 6,100 likes, and 470 shares. I turn off notifications again because the unending buzzing practically burns my phone.

People leave all sorts of comments. Most are good, like, "Wow, dolphins are so awesome," and "That's so cool to see animals helping each other." Exactly my feelings. Lots of people liked those comments too, but some gave them a thumbs-down. Who would be so negative as to dislike a comment about how awesome a dolphin is? What surprises me the most is that some of the comments are just mean or nasty. I don't get people. A manatee would never squash someone's happy, positive thoughts. Another reason manatees would make better people than people, if you ask me.

At school I don't look at my phone. Our school's policy is no phones and they're pretty strict about it, but I can't help feeling like a hot-air balloon stretching against its lines, waiting to fly into the sky. I'm sitting on a huge secret. Tens of thousands of people have seen this video and know about the amazing dolphin rescue, but everything around me is still normal.

I can't wait for science class for once. We're going to meet with Ms. Amato to talk about our progress on our project, and we'll tell her about our plans to feature the dolphin and the manatees in a public service announcement.

Ms. Amato looks up over her glasses at the three of us. We're seated around her desk. "Where are you on your project?"

I look to Deion and Amelia—they usually tumble all over themselves to speak up. Surprisingly, they look at me. I almost turn behind me to see if there's someone else in our group I'd forgotten about.

I blink a few times. "We have a video of a dolphin saving a group of manatees from a boat."

"Excuse me?"

"It's totally wild," Deion says. "This dolphin is all, like, you're not getting anywhere near my manatee friends." He splays his arms out dramatically.

"A boat was about to hit the manatees," Amelia explains, "and the dolphin risked its own life to jump in front of it."

"The dolphin saved the manatees from getting hit," I add.

"That's so unusual," Ms. Amato says. "I'd love to see it."

"It's online." I tell her the site and Ms. Amato pulls it up.

Her eyes widen. "It's quite popular. You have over forty-seven thousand views."

The three of us stare at one another. Deion mouths a silent *whoa.* Amelia is stunned into silence for once.

"Really?" I squeak.

Ms. Amato plays it and we all watch the now-familiar scene—the manatees moving along, the boat speeding in, and the dolphin throwing itself in front of the boat. I only halfway pay attention because the numbers of views and likes mesmerize me.

The idea that almost fifty thousand people have seen this video and heard my voice is unreal.

“This is remarkable,” Ms. Amato says. “How do you plan to use the video for your project?”

“We want to talk about the dangers of boats to manatees, and this video will be really dramatic,” I say.

Ms. Amato nods and she taps her pen against her face. “I’d like to put you in touch with my former professor at the University of Miami, Dr. Elena Martin. She specializes in dolphins.”

“A dolphin doctor? Does she squeak Dolphin?” Deion says.

Ms. Amato’s face grows stern. “Dr. Martin is a real, working scientist. You’ll need to be serious when talking to her and not waste her time.”

Deion gulps and shrinks. “I’m sorry, Ms. Amato. Why do we need to talk with her?”

“The dolphin shouldn’t be this far upriver. Dr. Martin could work with the FWC to rescue the dolphin and bring it back to the ocean.” Ms. Amato turns to her computer and starts to type. “You can help them by letting them know where and when to find the dolphin. And she can probably answer questions for your project too.”

My eyes grow wide. A cold feeling of dread seeps through

me. I'm not ready to talk to real live adults, especially marine biologists, and I definitely don't want to give up the dolphin's location. It seems happy in the river, playing with Missy, Sunny, and the other manatees. If I rat out the dolphin to some scientists, they'll separate a beautiful friendship.

"Sure, we can do it," Amelia says with a wide smile. "We know exactly where to find it. It shows up near Becca's and my docks most days."

I glare at Amelia. Doesn't she know how traitorous she's being to Missy and Sunny?

She looks at me quizzically. "What?"

My eyes cut to Ms. Amato. I can't talk about it here, not in front of our teacher, who's looking at me curiously. Her eyes soften. "Are you worried about the dolphin?"

"Yes. Sort of. I mean . . ." I lapse into silence. I can't explain why I think the dolphin would be happier staying with the manatees. There's a real friendship between the animals.

"The dolphin should be fine for a little while in the river," she says, misunderstanding my worried look, "but it can't stay for the long term. Dolphins aren't meant to live in fresh water.

Salt water keeps their skin healthy, and it's better to have it to rejoin its pod."

She's probably right, but I don't want her to be. Missy and Sunny need their protector, and she did say the dolphin will be fine for a while.

I'm beginning to think I made a mistake making this video public. I don't want scientists to come and tell us what to do. Amelia was right—we should have saved it for the PSA. When I made it public, at most, I thought city council members might see it and slow down the festival idea. But now Missy and Sunny could lose their dolphin friend because of me.

Over dinner, I tell Mom and Dad about the video getting all those views. Dad puts down his iced tea and says, "Hmm. If this video's getting a lot of interest, we should use it to get people interested in the boat festival. Imagine." He fans out his arms. "Show the video of the jumping dolphin and cut to a girl on a wakeboard doing a similar spinning move . . . Come see the excitement on Florida's Nature Coast. Even the dolphins are psyched for the festival!"

I groan inwardly. How can Dad see the same video and

think so differently? He doesn't even make the connection that it's boats like his that are endangering the manatees. "Dad, that's . . . not right."

He smiles. "It's just an idea, honey. I'm glad your video is getting a lot of attention."

I frown. He doesn't get it at all. He could listen to me if he wanted to, but he just doesn't care.

17

When I wake up in the morning, I turn on my phone.

My jaw drops.

Overnight, the video has reached 274,000 views and 11,900 shares.

I'm in complete shock. The numbers are so large, I can't even wrap my head around them. My school has 600 students, and our town is about 5,000 people. I'm not going to try to do the math, but a lot more people than my town's entire population have seen the video.

I go downstairs. I only have ten minutes before the bus comes, and Mom's made me one of my usual breakfasts, yogurt with fruit and honey. Dad sits at the island with his laptop and a strangely eager expression. "Your video is blowing up," he says.

"I know. I can't believe it."

Dad's eyes have a disturbing gleam. "I've got a great idea."

I have a feeling I won't like it. "What is it?"

"You'll see." He smiles and types away on his laptop. I come around to see what he's doing. As I look over his shoulder, he hits send on a post from his business account. He's posted the video and a caption:

Come see the extraordinary dolphin that saved the manatees. Call the number below to arrange riverside seats to one of nature's most unusual friendships.

My vision briefly grays out as I read those words. "Dad, you're inviting strangers to our house to see the dolphin?" I manage to croak. "Why would you do that?"

Mom looks up. "You're inviting strangers to our home?"

"Don't worry, I didn't put our address on the Internet. I'll screen the calls," Dad says. His phone rings, and he holds up a finger. "Hello . . . yes, this is he." He walks to the family room. "Which station are you with? Of course, I watch you all the time. Hold on, I have another call coming in."

"Mom," I hiss. "What is Dad doing? I don't want strangers

to come to our house." All those people will drive Missy and Sunny away.

Dad paces back and forth on the phone, giving out directions to our house and dock. Mom, glancing at Dad with an exasperated look, says, "I'm sure it'll be fine. I'll talk with him. Finish your breakfast and get your bag together. I'm not driving you to school again if you miss the bus."

I finish the morning scramble, gobbling up the rest of my yogurt and scooping up my backpack, but the whole time, I worry about Dad's sketchy plans. He's fielding more than one call at a time and taking notes on the back of an envelope. Missy, Sunny, and the dolphin don't even show up every day. What're people going to do, camp out in our backyard?

At school, when I get to the courtyard where we hang out before first bell, kids who haven't ever talked to me come up to me.

"Ms. Manatee!" says one boy, a tall kid named Mark who plays basketball. "High five!" He holds up his hand in the air, and I tap it tentatively.

"You're going viral, Becca," Emma says. She's one of the

popular girls whose talent is swishing her long brown hair. Her eyes are bright and her smile is wide.

I want to shrink from all this attention. I wonder who told everyone it was me who put up the video. This is not what I signed up for.

Amelia stands with a huddle of kids at one of the metal picnic tables. "This dolphin comes by our houses a lot. It plays with the manatees and is so awesome," she says. "We're working on teaching it some tricks. I told Becca she should make the video public after she showed it to me."

My mouth falls open. The others hang on her every word.

She smiles when she sees me. "Oh, here's Ms. Manatee herself." She puts her arms around my shoulder and jostles me into the circle of kids so now they're all staring at me.

"You're Internet famous," a guy says.

"Are you going to go on TV?" another girl asks.

My heart races and I sputter. "It's . . . I . . ." Finally, I manage to put together a sentence. "It's not about me. It's the manatees that are in danger." There, I said it. The kids stare at me as if I'm speaking a foreign language.

A boy pipes up, "What's the secret to making a video go

viral? None of my posts get more than a few hundred likes."

Deion elbows his way into the group. "Can I get your autograph?" he says, somehow managing to make fun of everyone around us while making me feel like a celebrity at the same time.

Amelia steps in front of me, holding up a hand. "Nuh-uh. I'm her manager. Autograph requests go through me."

"I thought I was her manager," Deion says.

I shrink back. I'm glad their playful bickering is taking attention away from me, but I'm still the focus of attention. When it's time to go to first period, I'm a jumble of emotions. Having Deion and Amelia by my side, running interference with the hordes of other students, is a huge relief. But Missy and Sunny are getting lost in the shuffle.

It's early Saturday morning, and I can't help checking the stats as soon as I wake up.

I inhale sharply.

Almost one million views! Or 987,558, to be exact, and the numbers are changing before my eyes. I look around my bedroom, the ceiling, and the window overlooking the old oaks and the river. This is surreal. My voice has been heard almost a million times. The number is so large, it doesn't compute. I open a couple of apps and see it's a trending topic on both.

I'm eating a bagel downstairs, still trying to wrap my thoughts around the number of views this video has gotten, when the doorbell rings. I never like answering the door, but neither Mom nor Dad is nearby. Mom's upstairs and Dad is out in the yard. I peek out the window to see if it's the UPS truck that I can safely ignore. Instead, parked in our driveway is a white truck with Channel 5's call sign, WKPP.

I want to hide, but a woman with sleek blonde hair and gobs of makeup leans over and looks through the glass by our front door, her face popping up like a genial clown. She smiles and waves at me, so I can't slink away like I was planning to.

I open the door.

"I'm Pamela Marks, from WKPP. Are your parents at home? Are you the girl who filmed the viral video?"

I stare at her, my mouth drying out. "One moment." I close the door in her face and run-walk to Mom and Dad's bedroom. "Mom, there's a TV reporter at the door."

Mom steps out of the bathroom with a bathrobe on and a towel around her head. "Dad mentioned she was coming, but I thought it was going to be later."

"Why's a reporter here?"

"It's exciting to have a viral video, so she wanted to interview us."

I don't like this at all. "I'm not talking to a reporter."

"You don't have to," Mom says. "Why don't you go find Dad?"

I head down the stairs of our house and out the back. Dad's tooling around his boat tied to our dock. When I tell him the reporter is here, he wipes his hands on his shorts and hurries around to the front of the house. I stay behind at the dock, on the lookout for Missy, Sunny, or the dolphin.

Pretty soon, Dad comes back with the reporter and the cameraperson in tow. I move off our dock as they approach. They set up so Dad stands in front of the river, calm and beautiful.

"Pamela Marks, WKPP, reporting from the backyard of local resident Eric Walker. How does it feel to have a video your daughter filmed go viral?"

My insides go jellylike. It hits me that this story is going to go on TV too. Somehow the Internet feels anonymous, but with TV, there'll be images of our house and Dad.

"I'm very proud of my daughter, who took the video and shared it. It's incredible to see the dolphin spinning in the air in front of the boat," Dad says. I perk up. Oh, good. Dad's going to talk about how boats shouldn't speed where manatees could be around. He's so personable. People will definitely listen to him. "It's an exciting cross-species friendship," he says. "We'll be opening our backyard for visitors to see this special friendship for themselves. Our town is a great place to visit to see sights like this."

As Dad talks, my hope curdles. He's inviting people to our backyard! And why isn't he talking about boats hitting manatees? Now he's talking about his boating festival. I edge past the reporter and cameraperson and hurry back to the house.

After the TV crew leaves, I storm into the study, where Dad's answering calls and taking notes. "Dad, why did you do that?"

He holds up his finger, but then changes his mind after seeing the look on my face. "Excuse me, may I call you back later?" He puts down the phone.

"Dad, how could you?" I say, trying not to let my voice crack. "Why are you inviting the world to our backyard?"

Dad looks at me with a slightly puzzled expression. "Becca, this is a once-in-a-lifetime opportunity. We can get our town on the map, and I can help build this into a place that draws people from all over."

"But Missy and Sunny are going to get scared away. It's too much." I'm not sure I'm making the right argument. "You didn't even ask me what I thought."

Dad looks taken aback. His brows furrow. "I'm sorry I didn't ask you. I know this must be a lot for you."

Mom steps into the study. "Everything all right?"

"Yes." "No." Dad and I answer at the same time.

"I was so excited by Becca's viral video, I didn't think about how it would affect her." Dad is saying all the right things, but it doesn't feel like he means it. "But you'll see, Becca, this is a good thing for our family and our town. We'll make some money from the people who come visit us and we can donate the proceeds to help the manatees."

"You're going to charge people to come to our yard to see the dolphin and manatees?"

"Not just to see them from our yard. I'll take them on a boat ride, like a river cruise." His face brightens. "You could come along and be a guide. You know so much about the manatees. Hold on, another call's coming in." He answers the phone and walks away, talking to another reporter or blogger or someone who wants to find out more about the amazing dolphin

I stare at him, shocked into silence. He's known me my whole life and he knows nothing about me. I turn and rush out of the study and up to my room.

19

The rest of the day goes by in a blur. TV reporters, neighbors, and random strangers show up at our house. Dad is in his element, all jovial and acting like the ringmaster of a circus, while Mom hangs out in her studio, tuning out the crowd. I hide in my room and see some texts from Amelia and Deion. I can't deal with them now, so I turn off my phone. If I don't see what's happening, maybe it'll go away. The one small consolation I have is that Missy, Sunny, and the dolphin haven't been back, probably staying far away from the commotion, so they're safe for now.

I'm lying on my stomach on my bed, trying to read a library book. It's a retelling of the King Arthur myth, and I usually love rereading my favorite books, like slipping on a pair of comfy shoes. But the words swim in front of my eyes, and I can't help thinking about what's going on outside in our yard.

A knock on my bedroom door startles me.

I think about ignoring it, but it's probably Mom, and I could use a friendly face, so I say, "Come in."

Amelia rushes in.

"Oh, hey." I sit up. I'm so happy to have a friend to complain about the circus outside with—something I wouldn't have expected even a few weeks ago. My smile slips when I see her stormy expression.

"What were you thinking?" she practically hisses. "You have no right to make this all about you. The video's for our science project. Deion and I are part of this too." She waves at the scene in our backyard. "You're so hypocritical. You talk about protecting the manatees when my dad fixes up a few Airbnbs, but *your* dad goes and invites the whole town."

I reel as if physically hit. "It's not my fault it went viral. I don't want any of this. I wish we could go back to what we were doing, just the three of us."

"Yeah, well, Deion's mad too," she says. "You would've known if you'd checked your phone, but it seems like you're too good to answer our texts."

Tears threaten to leak out. "I turned off my phone. I couldn't deal with it anymore. Why's Deion mad?"

"Same reason I am. We're a team and you're acting like you're the only one who matters."

My insides feel hollowed out, scraped clean. She and Deion have gotten it all wrong. The last thing I ever want is to be the focus of attention. "I hate what this has become. I can't help what my dad does." I can't even explain myself correctly.

She sighs and slumps down. "My dad's out there handing out flyers for his Airbnbs."

A brief hope flares that she might understand after all, that we can bond over this. "What do you think of that?"

Amelia frowns. "I don't know. This is good for his Airbnbs, but I'm not sure these people are the kind who care about manatees." She sits down on the chair by my desk. "I wish you hadn't made the video public the way you did. You complicated everything."

"Me too," I say.

"Yeah, well, it's too late now." Her face clouds up. "I've got to go." She pushes up from the chair and bolts out of the room.

I stare at the door that closes behind her and drop my head into my hands.

I turn on my phone. Maybe Amelia's wrong about Deion. I can't believe he would be mad or hold a grudge. He was excited when the video first started going viral. I ignore the thousands of notifications and go to my texts. I look up his last message: *Hello, anybody there?*

I write back. *I'm sorry. I turned off my phone.* I swallow hard and call him over video. I have to say it in person.

After a long moment, he connects.

I'm relieved, but nervous. "Hello." I give him an awkward wave.

"Yo." He tilts his head and looks at me like he's examining a virus under a microscope. "You look the same, Ms. Manatee, for someone who's a celebrity now."

I feel like I'm constantly apologizing, and it's not even my fault things have gotten out of control. "I'm still the same, Deion." It feels good to say that.

"I saw your dad on TV."

I cringe. I'd rather not be reminded of what's going on in my backyard. "That wasn't my idea. Are you mad at me?"

Deion's eyes shift away. "Nah. Why would I be mad at you?"

"Amelia said you were."

"Don't go believing everything you hear about me." He doesn't look at me when he says that, which makes me think he's not telling me the truth.

"Do you want to come over on Monday after school? We could work on our project." The science project isn't due for a few weeks, but I want to make sure Deion's not mad at me. I can't even believe I have the courage to invite him over.

He looks off the screen like he doesn't want to talk to me anymore. "I don't think it'll work with what's going on over there. Sunny and Missy won't show up."

I deflate. He's right. I need to convince Dad to shut down the tourist trap, but good luck to me trying to change Dad's mind about something.

"I gotta go," Deion says, his face serious.

We say bye and hang up. I flop back on my bed and stare at the ceiling. I said I was sorry, and he said it was fine, but it doesn't feel like we're good.

How did I get to this point? All I wanted was to let the city council know about how dangerous speeding boats are to manatees. It was never about me, but now I feel trapped in a glass cage, on display, with a horde of strangers laughing, pointing, and whispering about me. To make things worse, Dad's trying to make money from it, Amelia's angry, and Deion's disappointed. And to top it off, scientists are going to take the dolphin away, leaving Missy and Sunny alone.

My stomach starts to ache. Everything I do backfires. I should stay away from everyone and everything. I've never felt more alone and hopeless.

20

By late afternoon, the people who stopped by to see the dolphin and manatees have left, disappointed but clutching flyers for Mr. Carlson's Airbnbs. Our backyard is finally free of reporters, sightseers, and stragglers. Only my dad and Amelia's dad are left, chatting by some old oaks. I head to the dock to look for Missy and Sunny. Maybe now that it's calmer, they'll come back.

My feet creak on the wooden deck, and the water slaps gently against the pilings. Across the river, on the wild side, an anhinga sits on a low arching branch. I've always loved these birds, with their snakelike necks. When they swim in the water, most of their bodies are underwater with only their heads and necks sticking out, like snakes about to pounce.

I take a deep breath and let it out slowly, trying to allow

myself to relax. I scan the water for any manatee footprints, but nothing. Figures. Missy's smart enough not to bring her newborn baby someplace with a horde of gawking, loud people.

After fifteen or twenty minutes, I head back to the house. As I'm walking between the old oaks, Dad's and Mr. Carlson's voices drift over. I duck behind a tree. I don't feel like talking to Dad or saying hello to Mr. Carlson.

"Big vote at the city council meeting, huh?" Mr. Carlson says. I perk up and strain to hear their conversation. "They're voting on your festival idea, right?"

"Yeah," Dad says, "but it's just a formality."

"Really?"

I press my lips together. I'm not sure what he means by "it's just a formality," but it doesn't sound good.

"The festival's a go, because the mayor's all for bringing in tourism," Dad says. "The council has to go through the motions of holding a public hearing and listening to public comments, but it's a done deal."

My heart sinks. Whatever I or anyone else says won't make a difference, and Missy and Sunny are in trouble. I want to pop out from where I'm hiding and protest, but I'm rooted like the tree I'm leaning against. If it were just Dad, I'd try to get him to see my point of view, even though he didn't listen to me last time I brought up Missy and Sunny. But there's no way I'm going to make my case against his boat festival in front of Mr. Carlson. They move back to the house, and I lean against the tree. I pull at a piece of Spanish moss, dry and scratchy in my hands.

I close my eyes in frustration. I really need to talk to Dad. This has got to stop.

I'm about to go inside to confront Dad about the city council meeting when a text comes in from Deion. *Check this out!*

I click the link and it's an article about the newest meme that's spreading around the web—and it involves Missy and the dolphin! I read the article.

The latest meme that has taken the internet by storm has been dubbed the Dolphin Block. The image of a dolphin jumping into the air in front of a motorboat to protect a couple of manatees in the boat's path comes from a video posted by a user named Ms. Manatee a few days ago. This "blocking" meme has taken off for any situation that involves blocking or protecting someone or something, and it's all the rage. The memes are spreading even wider than the original video.

The picture used for the meme is a screenshot from my video of the moment the dolphin spins in the air, and people overlay words on it. They label the manatees, the dolphin, and the boat. None of them have anything to do with what's actually going on in the original video. In one, someone labeled the manatees *Your favorite TV show*, the dolphin *The fans*, and the boat *TV execs*. Another one labeled the manatees *The amazing singer*, the dolphin *The* Voice *Judge*, and the boat *The Other* Voice *Judge*. And it goes on and on, with athletes who make a great save, celebrities fighting over love interests, political protesters, and more.

I can't believe it. I keep scrolling and meme after meme pops up. I search #dolphinblock on two or three different apps and see a ton of memes, but I know there are even more that aren't using the hashtag. Each time the same image comes up. Some of the memes are really funny.

Having the video go viral was already too much, and now to see Missy, Sunny, and the dolphin used like punch lines in a thousand jokes makes me sick. They've become another thing to make someone laugh, without anyone paying attention to the real beings whose lives are in danger.

I text Deion. *Ugh. Thanks for letting me know.*

Then I text Amelia. *Can I come over?*

After a moment, she replies, *How about we meet at my backyard?*

Okay, I'm outside. I walk over to her backyard, picking my way through the ferns and palm trees.

Amelia skips down the steps of her house and slows down as she approaches me with a half frown. "What do you want to talk about?"

Seeing her hostile look gives me a sinking feeling. Somehow, without knowing it, she's become my friend. A real friend I care about, and I can't stand it that she's mad at me. I need to try to explain it to her again. "None of this is my fault. I can't control what happens on the internet."

Her expression doesn't change. She sighs heavily. "You put the video out without talking to us. Then you act like you're too good for us, not even texting me or Deion. Your dad was on TV bragging about you and didn't mention us."

I stare at her. "I told you, it's not like that," I protest. "My dad doesn't listen to me. I was off my phone because it was too much for me."

Amelia furrows her brow. "We're your friends. You didn't have to hide from us. At least I thought we were friends." Amelia whirls and stomps away back to her house, crunching leaves and twigs underfoot.

I open my mouth to call her to come back, to try to explain myself some more. I blink rapidly, trying not to cry. I heave a deep breath and slump down to the ground, burying my face in my hands. Everything's falling apart.

After several long minutes and deep breaths, I push myself up and head back to the house. I need to talk to someone. Somebody who's not Mom or Dad, who gets it about the manatees. I pull out my phone and call Grandma.

"Hello, Becca," she answers in her chipper voice. "How are you?"

I wonder if she's heard about the video going viral. She only uses her phone to make calls and even though I've taught her how to use Facebook a thousand times, her understanding of it is sketchy. Every time I go over, I need to help her reset her tablet, or find a missing app, or point out her twenty-three unread messages. Based on her cheery tone of voice, I'm guessing she doesn't know about how far the video has spread or the memes.

"Not so good," I say. "Can we go kayaking tomorrow?"

"Of course. What's the matter?" I can hear the worry in Grandma's words.

"I'll explain tomorrow. I need to get away."

"I'll come by and pick you up in the truck tomorrow at eight, and we'll head to the campground." She used to work at the FWC as a state park ranger. She loves kayaking and has taken me plenty of times. I need that peaceful, unspoiled nature now.

After saying good-bye, I push myself up from the ground, brushing off the leaves and dirt. I walk back to the house, already feeling better. The thought of facing Dad about the "done deal" festival causes me to pause and my heart to race. I don't want to talk to him now with my thoughts in such a jumble. I'll see Grandma tomorrow and then figure out how to deal with Dad.

21

It's Sunday, but my sleep app wakes me at seven thirty. I need to see Grandma and get out on the water. We're not going where Missy and Sunny hang out, but there's a good chance we'll see other manatees. I don't even check my phone to see how many views the video's gotten.

The truck pulls into the driveway. Mom's up already, working in her studio, so I stop by to say good morning. "I'm going kayaking with Grandma."

Mom looks up, though I can tell her mind is on the chair she's glazing. "Mmmkay. Don't forget to take your water bottle and grab something to eat before you leave. Will you be back by lunch?"

"Probably, but maybe Grandma'll take me out to lunch after. I'll let you know when we're done." I grab a chocolate chip granola bar from the kitchen and hurry out of the house and down the steps.

Grandma gives me a wide grin as I clamber up in her waiting truck with two kayaks lashed to the roof. "What's happening?"

"You're happening," I say, but the stress of the last few days comes crashing back. I slump in the seat, prop my elbow against the window, and rest my forehead on my hand. "A lot, and it's too much."

Grandma looks over at me sympathetically. "What is it? Classes? Friends? You look like you're holding up the weight of the world."

I sigh. "It's the manatees." I explain about the viral video, how Dad's pushing for a boat festival that's just going to bring more boats to the area, and how the memes are using the dolphin and manatees to entertain people.

"Aren't memes fun and won't they raise awareness?" she asks.

"But people aren't using it to raise awareness," I say. "They're just using the image to make a joke or talk about their favorite TV show. It's not even about Missy, Sunny, or the dolphin anymore."

"I'm sorry, sweetie. Tell you what, all of that is a bunch of noise. Where we're going, you'll be able to hear yourself think and you'll figure things out." She gives me a warm smile and turns up the volume on the radio.

I smile back uncertainly. I really could use some help to deal with all this intensity, but I wonder if the kayak trip will really help me take my mind off my worries.

Left, right. Left, right. I push my paddle in and out of the water on each side of my kayak, following Grandma in her kayak ahead. Every once in a while, water from the paddle splashes onto my arms or legs. I'm wearing my swimsuit under shorts and a T-shirt, a cap, sunglasses, and a life jacket. We glide through the smooth, still waters of the Chassahowitzka River, but my mind is anything but calm.

The memes bouncing around the net keep popping into my head. They're exactly the distraction I worry about, because if I'm thinking about them, for sure everyone else is too. Then there's Dad and Mr. Carlson making a circus of our backyard, inviting everyone and their cousin to a sea-life show. The city council meeting coming up where they're going to approve the boat festival that'll bring more boats to the springs. Dad hasn't paid any attention to what I have to say. Amelia is hardly talking to me, and I'm not sure about Deion. And worst of all, Missy and Sunny are in danger every day, and it'll only get worse.

I paddle as hard as I can, as if I could bury my troubles in the river with each stroke.

"Whoa," Grandma calls. "Since when did you become an Olympic kayaker? Slow down and enjoy the scenery."

I heave a sigh and stop paddling. As I drift along, I blow a dangling strand of hair off my face. How am I supposed to enjoy the scenery with Missy's and Sunny's lives in danger? We glide under a dead branch and near a tricolored heron. On the other side of the river is a tree filled with turkey vultures. It sure would be nice to sit on top of a tree looking down on the world with your buddies, not having to worry about boat strikes or viral videos and memes.

The old oaks interspersed with palm trees slowly slide by. The banks are a tumble of fallen logs, tall grasses, ferns, and brambles.

We're heading to a small cove where we've found manatees

before. We make our way in, looking out for the telltale signs of manatee footprints or their noses coming up for air.

Nothing.

We move on. A splash catches my attention.

"It's a mullet," Grandma says. "You shoulda seen the mullet runs we used to get when I was a girl. We'd sit in a boat and the mullet would swim by for half an hour."

I smile at the thought of Grandma as a kid in a boat on this river. "Tell me about how you used to catch crabs."

"I've told you a hundred times," she says with a chuckle.

"Tell me again."

"Well, my brothers and I used to catch crabs and toss them into our small open boat. When we dragged ourselves into the boat afterward, the most important thing was to make sure the crabs didn't grab ahold of our feet or fingers. If they did, there was nothing that could convince the crabs to let go, other than dangling them back over the water." She smiles. "Either we caught the crabs, or the crabs caught us."

I wonder if I could just pop into the water and catch crabs. I think I'd be too paranoid about alligators.

"The mullet's probably why the dolphin's in the river,"

Grandma continues. "Dolphins'll chase their food into fresh water."

"If dolphins come into the river to chase their food, it should be okay for them to hang around here, right?" It makes sense to me that nature wouldn't make an animal do something that would hurt itself.

"It's not good for the dolphin to be in fresh water," Grandma says. "When I was working as a park ranger, we came across a dolphin once in the river that had stayed too long, and it was covered with all sorts of skin sores and lesions."

Skin sores sound awful, but I bet that was just a dolphin that was already sick. Missy and Sunny's dolphin friend looks perfectly healthy.

The tide's coming in, so the ripples of water are going against us, making it harder to kayak, but we continue to paddle. The sun makes my skin prickle, and the breeze smells of dirt and moss and fish; water drops splash me as I dig my paddle into the river.

I set my jaw and paddle even harder.

A loud motor roars behind us. Grandma and I scoot closer to the riverbank. A couple of men in tank tops and cargo shorts standing on a scallop boat zoom by, staring at us impassively. A few moments later, their wake rocks us from side to side.

I glare at the disappearing boat. “Aren’t there speed limits here?” I ask.

“We’re still under winter rules, which means twenty-five miles per hour in this section of the river,” she says. “That boat was going a lot faster than that.”

My heart sinks. People don’t even pay attention to the speed limits that exist. Twenty-five miles an hour already seems awfully fast—and dangerous—for manatees.

An hour later, we reach our turning point. The landscape has changed dramatically since we started, with only cabbage palms and old leather ferns lining the riverbanks. Instead of the previous lush and crowded greenery, it’s a strange and lonely landscape. Grandma says it’s from global warming and rising seawater bringing more salt water into the mouth of the river, killing most of the plants except the palm trees.

Grandma glances over with a grin and points out a bald eagle across the river.

My eyes widen. A few yards behind her is the small dark snout of a manatee coming up for air. I motion and mouth, *Manatee!*

I move closer and we peer into the water. There it is. A huge manatee, bigger than my kayak grazes at the seagrass below us. It's a bit murky, but with my polarized sunglasses, I can see its large oval shape.

My heart floats out of my body. No matter how many times I see manatees, whether it's Missy or her baby or another one, it feels like the first time. The gentle giants, moving so peacefully underwater, unaware of our human problems and hurry, make me want to jump up and dance. This one's so big, I feel like a tiny blip next to it.

Grandma says, "Becca, you always bring us luck. What's happening, right?"

"You're happening, Grandma." I grin.

As we watch the manatee graze by our kayaks, it hits me. All this time with the viral video, I've been thinking only about myself—what people think of me and how awful I felt when Amelia and Deion misunderstood me. I was mad that no one was thinking of the manatees, but I wasn't much better.

"Grandma, I need these manatees to be all right"—I blink away a tear—"and I need to fix things with my friends."

The manatee moves away, and Grandma paddles closer to me. "I think you know what to do," she says.

A great blue heron glides down to the water in front of me, ripples fanning away as it lands.

I let out a ragged sigh. I do know. I have the power to make a difference, and I won't let my fears of speaking out stop me from helping the manatees. But first things first.

22

On our way home, I ask Grandma, "Can we go back to your house, and can I invite some friends over?" I don't know if Amelia and Deion will want to see me, but I have to try to reach them. The thought of going home to a street lined with cars, reporters, and hordes of sightseers makes me shudder.

Grandma smiles. "Of course. I'll check with your parents, but I don't see why not."

I text Amelia and Deion. *I'm so sorry about everything going on at my house. I have an idea, and I need your help. Can you come over to my grandma's place?*

At Grandma's house, I sit at her kitchen table with a fresh-squeezed lemonade and wait to hear back from my friends. Soon enough, they say they can come, and I share the address.

I check my video stats for the first time in over a day. If I were at home I probably would've refreshed it over and over, caught up in Dad's excitement about the video, or in my own anxious thoughts.

When I open the app, it takes a moment to register.

The video's been watched over three million times.

I gasp. I don't even know how to think about a million views, and now it's three times that.

"What is it?" Grandma asks.

"It's my video." I show it to her. "I can't get over how many people have watched it."

"Your dad called this morning while you were out kayaking. The reporters would like to talk with you as the person who witnessed the dolphin saving the manatees."

I exhale deeply. Why Dad still thinks I want to talk to reporters is beyond me. The thought of facing them gives me the shivers. "I can't talk to reporters."

The doorbell rings, and it's Deion with his mom.

"Hello, I'm Patricia Walker," Grandma says.

"I'm Laura Williams." Deion's mother is tall and thin like Deion, with an easygoing smile.

I wave to Deion, who nods and joins me in the family room while Grandma and Mrs. Williams chat.

"What's going on?" Deion has a neutral expression.

"I've been thinking a lot about the video, but I want to wait until Amelia gets here so I can say it once." My heart pounds.

He considers me for a moment and nods. He flops down on the couch and pulls out his phone. I get up and pace around, not sure what to do while we're waiting. This isn't a comfortable silence. It's the opposite—a cringey one filled with nervous energy, at least for me. Deion doesn't seem to notice, tapping away at his phone.

As his mom leaves, Amelia arrives and comes into the family room with a closed-off expression.

"I'm glad you came." I steady my voice. "I'm really sorry about disappearing." I feel like I'm always apologizing, but it seems to be the right thing to do. "I didn't know how to deal with all the attention."

"It hasn't been easy for us either," Amelia says.

"I know," I say. "When you turned away from me, it hurt my feelings that you weren't there for me."

Amelia looks away.

Deion coughs and fidgets.

"But then I realized I was being selfish," I say. "The video blowing up messed us all up, but here's the thing: I want to get back to why I shared it in the first place. We have to warn people of the dangers of boats. We need to use it to stop the council from approving the festival."

"What does that mean for us?" Amelia asks.

"Let's make the PSA," I say, "but we do it our way. You've told me to let my personality show." I take a deep breath. This is it. I'm going to put myself out there. "I want you to interview me, and I'll talk about the dangers of boats to manatees." I keep going before I lose my nerve. "We can use the video, but explain it, so people understand what's going on."

Deion nods. "We use how popular the video's gotten to get people's attention."

"Yes," I say, "and we need to do it quickly, because the city council's about to approve my dad's boating proposal. If we can put out our video before then, maybe it'll change their minds."

"But the project's not due until after the city council

meeting," Deion says. "I've never finished a project before it's due."

I give him an exasperated look.

He holds up his hands. "Okay, fine."

Amelia leans back. "But how're we going to know that things won't get out of control again, or you won't hide away when things get tough?"

I stare down at my shoelaces, then look at Amelia and Deion. "I promise I won't disappear again. I'm not used to remembering I have friends."

Amelia blinks a few times and finally breaks into a crooked smile. "You better get used to the idea, 'cause we're not going away."

She nudges Deion, who says, "Yup. Not going away. You're stuck with us now. We're your barnacle buddies."

I could almost cry with relief and happiness, but instead I let out a ragged breath and smile.

"I have an idea," Amelia says. "Let's show the video we make to the city council at the hearing next week."

I stare at her. "But that means speaking up in person." Getting in front of the camera to do this new video will be hard enough. I won't be able to show it in person.

"That's the thing," Amelia says, "you can do it, and you'll be great at it. Plus, we'll be there too."

"But who'll listen to a kid?"

"Are you kidding me? You know so much about manatees, and it shouldn't matter what age you are," Amelia says.

"That's right," Deion adds. "Remember when Greta Thunberg talked to the United Nations and world governments? She's a kid too. You only need to face the city council."

A flutter goes through me. It's different from all the other times my insides have made themselves known, because now it's a twinge of growing excitement. I really can do this. Amelia's and Deion's smiling faces make it feel doable. I have my friends back, and we're doing it together.

"All right, let's do it."

23

We get right to work on the video.

"What do you want to say?" Amelia holds up her phone, ready to film me.

"I think we should focus on what the city council is deciding on," I say.

"We can look up what's on their agenda," Deion says.

"Look at you, Mr. Politics." Amelia puts down her phone. "How do you know that?"

He shrugs. "My mom had to go to the council last year when she was trying to get a playground put in the park by our house." He snorts. "The things my parents do for my little sister. Anyway, you can look up what they're going to discuss online and sign up to talk."

I gulp. This is getting too real. I pull up the city council's website and poke around until I find the agenda. "They're going to discuss a special event permit for the Winter Boating Extravaganza." I make a face.

"What kind of name is that?" Deion says.

"I know, right?" I say.

Amelia's crouched over my shoulder, reading. "Look, there's a place to write in ideas for new topics for future meetings." She turns to me. "Let's ask the city to enforce the speed limits for Jet Skis and boats."

That feeling of impending doom crashes down. "I'm not sure I can do this."

Amelia glares at me. "Yes, you can."

"I believe in you," Deion says with a grin.

I straighten up, their words pulling me up to the sky. "Okay, I'll sign us up to say something." My breath grows shallow as my fingers hover over the keyboard. A few clicks and I'll be committed.

I tap away at the computer, and in a few minutes, it's done.

"Now are we ready to video your big speech?" Amelia asks.

I take a breath. "Yes. I want to say my piece and we can cut to the video of the dolphin jumping in front of the boat."

She takes out her phone again. “Okay. Whenever you’re ready.”

We’re sitting on the couch, but this feels wrong. “This isn’t working. We need to be by the river at my house.”

“But isn’t there a mob there now?” Deion asks.

I furrow my brow. “You’re right. We need to be at the river with no one around, and if no one’s around, maybe Missy and Sunny will come back too.” It’s past time to talk to Dad. He needs to hear why what he’s doing at our house is making everything worse, but thinking about confronting him gives me a stomachache. But I miss Sunny and Missy and need to know if they’re all right. “Amelia, let’s go talk to our dads and ask them to send the people away.”

She twists her lips and stays silent for a long time. Finally, she says, “I know you’re right, but I don’t want to get my dad mad. He’s already in a bad mood all the time, fighting with Mom.”

I sigh. Everything is always complicated. “I’ll talk with my dad, but will you come with me?”

Deion smiles. “Like be your moral support. Yeah, sure.”

Amelia nods.

I call to the kitchen, "Grandma, can you drive us back home?"

When we arrive home, Grandma's truck barely squeezes through all the parked cars on either side of the street. A white truck with the FWC logo sits in our driveway.

I hop out and make my way to the backyard, where a dozen or so people crowd around the shoreline. A kid about our age throws a rock into the river, and I wince. A little girl squeals as she chases her scampering dog, and a couple on the dock peer into the water. Two boats are tied to our dock and another one putters in the river.

The only reason my head doesn't explode is because I'm pretty sure Missy, Sunny, and the dolphin are smart enough to stay away from this pandemonium.

I rush down to the river, with Amelia and Deion following. I spot Dad and Mr. Carlson talking to a woman and a man wearing greenish-khaki pants and tannish-khaki short-sleeved shirts. They look awfully official.

"Hi, Becca," Dad calls. "These are FWC officers who're here to look for the dolphin. They're organizing a recovery mission to capture the dolphin and release it back out in the Gulf."

I whip my head to look at the pair. My heart squeezes tight like it always does when I have to talk to a stranger, but I've had practice now at pushing through. "You can't . . . the manatees need their friend," I stammer. I look past them at the river. Luckily, as I guessed, there's no sign of the dolphin.

"It's done nothing but be a hero," Deion says.

I think quickly. "Can you just watch it for a while? Monitor how it's doing?"

The woman says, "That's actually part of our protocol. Once we find it, we will monitor it before taking further action."

"Okay." I smile uncertainly. Did I just win?

"When was the last time you saw it?" she asks.

I try to think. It was before the video went viral, which already seems like a million years ago.

Amelia tugs at my arm and moves her eyebrows up and down in an alarming fashion. I get the hint. "Excuse me, please," I say.

Amelia practically drags me to the dock, and my feet trip keeping up with her. Deion huddles close. "What's going on?" I hiss.

"Act natural," she says.

"How am I supposed to act natural if you're dragging me like you're kidnapping me?"

Amelia lets go and smiles brightly and waves to her dad talking with the FWC officers.

The three of us jostle one another as we walk down the dock.

"Look over there," she says in a quiet voice.

Out on the other side of the river, away from the boats, I see the manatee footprints. I'm sure they're Missy and Sunny. I gulp. They've gotten so used to coming here that now they're in danger, and it's my fault. It was because of my video that all these people are here. "We need to get these people out of here," I say. "They're going to ruin everything."

"I've got your back," Deion says. "What should we do?"

"We can't let people realize Missy and Sunny are here."

"How are we going to get them to leave, and the FWC people too?" Amelia asks. "And those boats?"

I don't know the answer, but I know I have to try. I stalk back to the bank, where Dad is still chatting with the FWC officers.

"Dad, can I speak with you?"

"Sure. Excuse me a moment, folks." Dad steps aside and puts his arm around my shoulder. "What's up, bug?"

I stare at him and my eyes tear up. "Dad, I've been trying to talk to you for a long time. I really need you to listen to me."

His eyes widen. "I'm listening."

All the words that've been swirling around in my head finally come together. "Please send all these people away. Missy and Sunny aren't going to come back until they leave." I bite my lip over the lie.

His face flickers. "It means that much to you?"

"Yes." My mouth feels dry, my heart pounds, but I keep going. "Having the video go viral is too much for me. There's no place to hide from it, and our home should be that place, for me and for the manatees."

Dad looks at the people trampling our yard. "Fine. I'll send them away." My heart is about to burst with joy. "I've got to work on my proposal for the council meeting anyway," he adds.

My heart settles back down in disappointment. "Can we talk about the festival?"

"Sure, bug. We'll talk later tonight."

Dad walks back to the FWC officers, who are shaking hands with Mr. Carlson. "Thanks, guys, I have your cards, and we'll be sure to call you if we see the dolphin." He says something to Amelia's dad in a low voice, and the two of them make their way among the people in our yards, herding them back to their cars or boats.

Amelia and Deion exchange triumphant grins, but mine is strained. These people can't leave soon enough.

When everyone finally leaves, the three of us hurry back to the dock.

Missy and Sunny are gone.

My shoulders relax.

"Now are you ready to make our video?" Amelia asks.

I shake my head. "Not now. Let's just sit for a moment."

Amelia and Deion sit next to me, our legs dangling off the dock. The wind blows through my hair and a mullet splashes the water. We got our small victory by getting rid of the people from our yards, and Missy and Sunny seem to be all right for now, but Dad's plan for a boating festival is still happening. I've got to convince him not to go forward with the project.

* * *

After my friends leave, I head to the office, my heart beating double time. Dad's on his laptop, a map of the bay and a bunch of papers spread on the desk.

He looks up over his glasses. "Becca bug, what's up?"

I perch myself on the chair-and-a-half in the corner, my knees bouncing. I usually like to curl up here to read, but this isn't a comfy read-a-thon. I come right to the point. "Do you have to push for a boating festival? Bringing all those boats here could hurt Missy, Sunny, and the other manatees."

Dad takes his glasses off. "Most of the boating events are going to take place in the bay, and I've told you we're going to follow the environmental regulations. That's what I'm working on right now."

My brows scrunch together. "But the manatees will be out in the bay too. There's also a dolphin there. Couldn't you do the festival in the summer, when the manatees aren't around?"

Dad shakes his head. "We want to do the festival when the tourists will be here. Becca, I don't have time to discuss this right now. Trust me. Your video has been a boon already to my business, and we can even use it to advertise the festival." He turns back to his laptop. "Now if you'll excuse me, I need to get this done for Thursday's city council meeting."

I stare at him. *It's a done deal* echoes through my head. Whatever Dad says about caring for the manatees or environmental reviews doesn't mean a thing.

24

It's Monday, and Ms. Amato's giving everyone time to work on their projects at school, so we're doing some final research before we put together our video.

"Listen to this," Amelia says. "One of the biggest threats manatees face is the loss of warm-water habitats."

"What's that mean?" Deion asks.

Amelia studies the article. "Manatees need to have warm water in the winter, but Florida's warm springs are disappearing because people are building new homes or pumping the water for farming."

"That's terrible," Deion says, "but it's not going to get people excited, and it doesn't have much to do with the boating festival."

"But look at this report," I say. "In Florida, the leading cause of death to manatees is boats." I wince when photos of manatees with boat scars show up on the screen. "Most adult manatees have some sort of scar from being hit by a boat." I've read this fact and knew it, but seeing picture after picture of manatees with their scars hits home. I think of sweet Sunny—a manatee who is unblemished and has never felt the pain and shock of being hit. But one day, maybe a year from now, or maybe three years from now, he might be struck by a speeding boat or Jet Ski.

"That's horrible." Deion looks as stricken as I feel.

"So are we meeting after school to do the video?" Amelia asks. "The city council meeting is in a few days."

I gulp. The pressure's building up, and I know we need to work on this video and get it together, but I don't know if we can pull it off. I'm petrified by the thought of presenting to the council. Dad's already said the decision's a done deal. And can I really go up against Dad's plans in front of the whole town?

"Let's do it, and we'll be ready," I say, trying to hide my doubts. I'll have the chance to make our case, but will it be enough?

* * *

We meet after school at the dock. I look around hopefully for Missy and Sunny or the dolphin, but no luck. They're not back. It doesn't matter, though. I've got enough footage of them from other videos we can splice together. All I need to do is introduce the problem in a way that will convince people to care.

Deion holds the phone ready to film me, but he's moving side to side, antsy as usual.

"Hold still," I say.

He puts down the phone and wiggles his entire body. "Okay, gotta calm down." He grins. "Can't have the camera operator be all jittery."

I laugh.

Amelia, who's been scanning the water for Missy and Sunny, turns to us. "This is serious business, guys."

I smooth my face back into serious mode. She's right, but I'm also starting to realize that it's okay to have fun too while doing this important thing. "I'm ready."

"I'm going to count down, and you start talking in five, four, three, two . . ." Deion holds up a finger to let me know I'm on.

I never thought I'd be doing this. I feel like I'm standing on a cliff about to jump into a lake far below. The idea is suddenly exhilarating. I take a deep breath and begin. "You've seen the video and the memes of the dolphin jumping in front of the boat about to hit the manatees. My name is Becca Wong Walker, and I took the video."

Deion gives me an encouraging nod. Amelia throws up two big thumbs-up and motions wildly. I'm going to take that as, *Keep going, you're doing great.*

"This dolphin did an extraordinary thing. We all know it. But what you may not know"—I glance at my friends, who both nod—"is there's a city council meeting about boats in the Two Brothers Springs area in three days, on March twenty-fifth. They're about to approve a boating festival scheduled for next winter that will bring tons of boats to the area. This could hurt the manatees. Please come out to let the council know you're worried about the manatees. A dolphin can't save the manatees by itself. We need your help."

A feeling of relief and exhilaration thrills through me. I did it!

Deion turns the video to Amelia, and she says, "Click on the link below for more information." She points down excitedly with both hands to the bottom of the screen, where we'll add a link.

The three of us are back in my room with the family laptop and my phone. We've worked all afternoon, taken a dinner break of fried rice and stir-fried chicken and snow peas, and now it's late. We've edited the footage of me in front of the river together with the original video and added links to a website we created with all sorts of facts about manatees and boats and information about the council meeting. I press publish and the new video goes live.

Deion slides down the chair like melted taffy. "I can't believe we worked so hard. What's the emergency?"

I glare at him. "The city council meeting is three days away and we need to get the word out so people care about it and come to it."

"How are we going to get people to watch this version of the video?" Amelia asks. "It's got"—she looks at the screen—"one view, and that's probably us."

Good question. I stare at this video. It took me all my

courage to turn the camera on me, to say my brief piece, and no one's going to listen. Story of my life.

Deion sits up, a sly smile working its way across his face. "Here, give me your laptop."

I look at him dubiously. "What're you going to do?"

"Do you trust me?" He turns on his most charming smile, which normally is most certainly not one to trust, but I've gotten used to his over-the-top persona masking what's underneath. "It's easier if I show you instead of explaining," he says.

Amelia shrugs, with a *don't look at me* expression.

"Fine." I push the laptop to Deion and he taps away at the keyboard. After a few moments, his eyebrows meet in deep thought and he presses the return button with a flourish. He hands the laptop to me.

Amelia and I crouch over the screen to see what he's done. We're still looking at our new video, but now the view counter is flipping like crazy, with the views hitting twenty, then forty and seventy. It's viral video 2.0.

"What are you, some kind of magic ninja hacker?" Amelia asks.

"Nah," he says. "I used the dolphin block meme, but for our own point." He clicks on a different tab and shows us what he did.

Deion has made his own #dolphinblock meme. On the boat, he typed the phrase *Internet hordes*. On the dolphin, he wrote *The real video you should see*, and on the manatees, he typed *The manatees*. He added a link to our new video.

I break into a smile. Deion is so original, always with a fresh take on things. It turns out teamwork and having friends make things so much better. "You used the meme to remind people the point of it all is to protect the manatees."

"You're welcome," he says with a grin.

"Thank you," I say.

25

Our new video isn't as popular as the original one, but it's gotten plenty of views in the three days since we posted it. With a half hour to go until the start of the city council meeting, the video has over 21,000 views, with the comment section on fire. I'm in the back seat of our car with Deion. Amelia's coming separately with her parents.

"It's nice of you kids to come see Dad talk about his boating festival proposal," Mom says.

Deion and I exchange looks. Since Dad wouldn't listen to me, I thought if he knew my plan, he wouldn't let me come. Now I realize that wasn't such a great idea. Dad will probably get really angry if I embarrass him by opposing him in public.

We turn onto the street for city hall.

The first sign this is no ordinary city council meeting is the long line of cars pulling into the parking lot. The second sign is the crowds of people on the sidewalk holding signs and chanting. I crane my neck to read them.

An older woman with frizzy hair holds up a sign that says, FLORIDIANS FOR BOATING RIGHTS: DON'T MESS WITH US BECAUSE WE'RE NOT MESSING WITH THE MANATEES. I can't believe there's actually a group that's promoting speeding boats. A large guy who reminds me of a friendly bear holds up a sign that says, TAKE THE DOLPHIN BACK HOME. He faces a much smaller man, who shouts, "The dolphin should stay if it wants to stay!"

We make our way to a parking spot and walk toward city hall's steps. We pass a woman with long, messy braids holding up a sign for the Citizens Concerned about the Connectors, who shouts, "No more toll roads! The manatees need their homes more than the developers do!" The toll roads aren't even on the agenda, but I guess all the publicity from the dolphin video brought everyone who cares about manatees out tonight.

Deion and I follow Mom and Dad as we push our way through the crowds and their chanting and signs.

"Can you believe this crowd?" Mom asks.

Dad looks around, shaking his head. "I'm impressed by this show of civic interest."

It's overwhelming. All these people came out because of something *I* did—first, my video of the dolphin, and now, the video asking them to be here.

We go through security and arrive at a large and stuffy room. The space hums with conversation and chairs scrape as people make themselves comfortable. I scan the room for Amelia. When we spot each other, she waves wildly at me, and I turn to Mom. "Can Deion and I sit with her?"

Mom nods. "Sure. Dad and I will be up front. He's on the agenda to present."

Deion and I wind our way to Amelia.

"I saved seats for you." She moves some papers and her mom's purse from the seats and we sit.

"Hi, Mr. and Mrs. Carlson," I say.

Amelia's parents smile. "So nice to see all these people interested in local politics," Mrs. Carlson says, "especially young folks like yourselves."

Deion gives me a look. All of a sudden, it sinks in. I'm going to speak in front of everyone: my parents, the Carlsons, and the council members. I don't know if I can do it. Maybe I don't have to speak after all. Maybe all these other people with their signs can do it for me. I'll just melt into my seat like a nice puddle of goo.

It's eight and a woman with graying hair held up in a bun calls the meeting to order. There's a bunch of preliminary stuff, which is super boring, and then she says, "Our first order of business is to discuss the proposal by Eric Walker, owner of Nature Coast Boats, to hold the Diamond Springs Winter Boating Extravaganza in January. We've posted the proposal on our website for the thirty-day comment period and are opening the floor today for public comments on the permits." She looks out at the crowd. "It's unusual to have such a turnout for one of our meetings. I understand we have a young lady to thank for it." She peers at her page and looks up. "Miss Becca Wong Walker, who happens to be the daughter of Mr. Walker."

I shrink down in my seat as Amelia and Deion both sit up straight. Deion waves and points at me, mouthing, *This is her!* The people around us look at me with interest and my face burns with heat.

"Mr. Walker, will you walk us through the highlights of your proposal?"

Dad walks up to the podium, smoothing the top of his hair, which is short, so I'm not sure what the point is. "Thank you, Chairwoman Leeds. A consortium of businesses I'm a part of proposes to host the Winter Boating Extravaganza. We hope this will become a yearly event to draw visitors who might otherwise head to other parts of Florida, like Orlando or Miami. Each year, we'll feature the latest motorized water sports equipment, such as electric-powered motor boards, sea scooters, and flyboards, along with wakeboard and tubing contests. The goal is to create something different and fun that appeals to younger people."

The chairwoman flips through a binder. "You'll need to go through the permitting process, from security to logistics and environmental impacts."

"Of course," Dad says. "We'll be happy to provide all the information you require." He goes on to outline all his research into how many people are expected to come, how much money they'll spend, and all his big plans.

When he's done, the chairwoman says, "We'll open the floor

to public comments. We'll hear first from those who've signed up in advance."

Gulp. That's me. She's going to call my name any second. I grip Amelia's hand.

"You can do it," she whispers.

The chairwoman calls up some guy. I don't hear who he is, because I'm busy trying not to puke from nervousness. Before long, his words seep into my brain. ". . . Floridians for Boating Rights. We advocate responsible boating." I pay attention, hoping this group will support some restrictions on the festival. He continues, "We're out on the water all year round and our members report increasing numbers of manatees from year to year, so clearly they're doing just fine. We strongly support the Winter Boating Extravaganza and look forward to spreading the word about it."

My heart sinks. It may be true there are more manatees these days, but they're still threatened by boats and development.

The next person called up is the girl we saw at the wildlife refuge, with Citizens Concerned about the Connectors. She talks about the problems with the proposed toll roads, which

I agree are a huge problem, but the chairwoman reminds her to stay on topic.

My heart starts drumming really hard. I'm not ready.

"Our next commenter is Becca Wong Walker." She looks at me over her glasses. "Our local celebrity, who brought all this attention to our town."

I push myself to my feet and walk awkwardly out of the seating area and to the front. As I pass Dad, he gives me a puzzled look.

"Hello." I clear my throat, which feels all scratchy. This is it. This is the moment I need to make my case.

I close my eyes. I don't think I can do this. I should just take my notes and run out the room and hide away for good.

But I can't hide anymore. I need to speak up for Missy and Sunny.

"My name is Becca Wong Walker, and I took the video of the dolphin jumping in front of the boat." A murmur runs through the room.

I feel like I could pass out. The whole room goes dim and lights up again. I grip the podium. An image of Missy and Sunny comes to mind. Sunny, the cute little baby manatee who's never been hit by a boat. If only he could grow up until a ripe old age and never get scarred or hit. It's him and his mama that I'm here for. A feeling of power and peace wells up in me. I can do this.

"The manatees follow their instincts, and every winter, they come back to our warm springs. If we hold the boating festival in the winter when the Gulf waters are cold, that's exactly when the manatees gather in the springs. Speeding boats are the number one killer of manatees in our area."

I look at the council members. Some of them look interested, some take notes, but one or two don't pay attention. I'm not reaching them. I'm not going to make a difference.

I start to tear up but push it down. I raise my voice, aware that it trembles slightly. "I'm here to speak up for the manatees, because they can't speak for themselves." I swivel around and look at the crowd and swing my arms to cover everyone. "We're the species with the supposedly large brains, but all we've done is build stuff, ride fast boats, and look for the next meme. We only think about ourselves and what makes us happy. The dolphin was better than that. It didn't think of itself when it risked everything to save its friends.

"Everybody loved the video of the dolphin and shared it over three million times. Let's be better, like the dolphin." I look over to my parents. Mom's staring at me with wide eyes, and Dad shakes his head slightly. I glance back at Amelia with her parents. I don't want to ruin things for her family or disappoint my parents, but Missy and Sunny need me.

I've got to believe I can protect Missy and Sunny without hurting the people I love.

Then a new idea comes to me. "Instead of doing the Winter Boat Extravaganza, could the city please do a manatee festival instead?"

A murmur fills the room. Dad tilts his head.

I continue before I lose my courage. "My friends, Amelia Carlson and Deion Williams, and I have researched manatees for school." I glance back at them. Amelia smiles, and Deion pumps his fist.

"In the summer, the manatees are spread all over Florida, the Gulf, and the Atlantic, so don't concentrate here until late fall. We can move the festival to early fall, and teach people about manatees and have booths, games, and music."

Now all the council members are paying attention.

"Let's bring this town together, but for the manatees."

From the crowd, Deion shouts, "Yeah! For the manatees!"

Amelia's voice joins in. "For the manatees!"

The other kids from our school in the audience take up the chant. "For the manatees! For the manatees!" Soon, the CCC girl and the scientists and more adults join in.

"For the manatees! For the manatees!" I break into a huge grin. It's like my viral video has gone viral in real life. The energy of the room is a tidal wave.

The chairwoman scrambles around until she finds a gavel. She brings it down, just like in a courtroom drama. "Order! Everyone come to order!" It takes several minutes, but eventually people quiet down. "We'll take a fifteen-minute break."

"For the manatees!" Deion sneaks in one last rallying cry.

If I weren't gripping the podium, I would probably collapse in a heap.

26

Everyone mills around during the break. Mom rushes over. "Becca, why didn't you tell us you were planning to speak?"

I study her expression. Is she mad at me?

"You were so brave," she says. "I'm proud of you."

A rush of elation and relief fills me. "Thanks." We hug and I look over her shoulder. "Where's Dad?" He's the one I'm worried about. I wonder how he took my public rebellion against his project.

Mom looks around. "I don't know. Maybe he's in the restroom?"

I can't help feeling hurt he didn't come over to me at the break. "I'd better go back to my seat."

"See you after the hearing," Mom says.

I join Deion and Amelia, a flurry of emotions inside, from elated to nervous and everything in between.

"High five!" Amelia and I exchange one. "You rocked."

"Ms. Manatee!" Deion and I fist-bump.

Mr. Carlson gives me a bemused look. "Quite a show you put on there."

"Um, thanks?"

Mr. Carlson turns to his wife. "You know, maybe we should rebrand our Airbnbs as an eco-destination. There seems to be a lot of manatee love here."

Mrs. Carlson takes his hand. "What a great idea. We can provide canoes and kayaks instead of Jet Skis at our rentals."

Amelia stares at her parents holding hands and smiles.

I glance at the door. Still no sign of Dad.

The meeting is called back to order. The chairwoman leans into the mike. "During the break, we received an unusual request. I'll let Mr. Walker explain."

Dad steps to the podium. I hadn't noticed when he came back to the room. What is going on?

"Thank you, Ms. Leeds," he says. "Given the recent proposal

by Ms. Wong Walker"—he glances at me and shoots me a smile—"our consortium is withdrawing our proposal for the Winter Boat Festival."

The room erupts in shouts, voices, and a general din. I'm not sure I heard correctly.

"We will be happy to work with any of the interested parties to retool our festival to focus on manatees and ecological awareness. I will work with boating operators to offer classes on safe boating practices and we'll have kayak excursions. And we'll consider other times of the year for the festival."

Amelia and Deion are hugging and shaking me. I'm so elated, I can't stop grinning. I made a difference. The rest of the meeting goes by quickly as many of the proposed comments are no longer relevant, though people do stand up to share their ideas for a manatee festival.

At the end of the meeting, I walk out, still dazed. Dad meets me in the hallway. "Becca, I knew you cared about the manatees and the dolphin, but it wasn't until you got up that I saw how truly passionate you are." He sits down on a bench, and I join him. "I see now how much pressure you've been under with the video going viral, and I'm sorry it went to my head, and I got carried away. I was so excited for my boat business I didn't think about you."

He takes my hands, and I pull them back. No way am I going to settle for holding hands when I can give him a huge bear hug instead. I move in for our hug, and he squeezes me back. After a good long time, we separate.

"I'm sorry I didn't tell you I was going to speak against the boat festival," I say. "Thank you for backing me up after all."

"Of course, bug." Dad shakes his head, but his smile betrays him. "You're something else."

"Looks like the two of you should've talked to each other before preparing rival presentations," Mom says.

"I suppose so." I grin.

Dad pulls me to my feet from the bench, and we walk down the hall with our arms around each other.

Amelia, Deion, and I bounce off one another as we make our way down the hall and out of city hall, the parents following behind. We run into Ms. Amato just outside at the top of the steps.

“Ms. Amato!” Deion says.

“Deion, Becca, Amelia.” Ms. Amato grins and we exchange fist bumps. “Y’all did great. Becca, I’m so proud of you. You did a great job speaking up for the manatees.”

My mouth hurts from smiling so widely.

“And Deion and Amelia, I can tell you two have worked really hard on this project too,” she says. Ms. Amato puts a hand on Deion’s shoulder. “I saw that meme you made to get people here to the meeting. Nice work.”

Deion beams. “Who knew science could be so fun?”

Ms. Amato laughs. “And that you can get serious when you put your mind to it.” She greets our parents and they chitchat. We reach the sidewalk, where a TV truck is parked outside. The reporter from WKPP, Pamela Marks, stands by the sidewalk with her microphone and camera crew.

“Ms. Wong Walker,” she calls out.

I look around. “Me?”

“Yes.” She gives me a confiding smile. “You’re the face of the new video that got everyone riled up to come to city hall. You’re the one who put our town on the map with the original video. May I ask you a few questions?"

My instinct is to shrink behind Dad or Mom, but I remember how I didn't dissolve in the meeting. I straighten up. "Okay." Then I pull my friends over. "It's not just me. These are my friends, Deion Williams and Amelia Carlson. We're a team, and we worked together on getting the word out."

Ms. Marks smiles. "Wonderful. The university and state scientists all agree the dolphin should be sent back to the Gulf. What do you think of that?"

I'm taken aback. Up until now I haven't had to take a stand on this. It seems to me the dolphin is just fine hanging out with Missy and Sunny. "I think . . ." I sigh. "I'm not a scientist. If they say the dolphin should return to salt water, then I believe them."

"People are listening to you now. You're known as Ms. Manatee. Will you post or say something to your followers about this?" the woman asks.

My eyes widen. I haven't thought of myself as having followers. My secret dream is to be a famous marine biologist with her own show, and it seems like part of this dream has come true. I'm a famous somebody with her own show. It feels . . . wonderful. I smile. People are listening to me. It's wild and unbelievable, yet true.

I smile. "Yes. My next episode will be a call to bring the dolphin back to the ocean."

27

Amelia, Deion, and I perch over the railing of the wooden walkway in the state park overlooking Two Brothers Springs. We're here with our families, though our parents and others have walked on ahead. In the coldest part of the winter, there were hundreds of manatees hanging around here waiting for the rest of Florida's waters to warm up. Now at the end of March, there are only a few stragglers.

The water is clear to the bottom. The moss hanging from the old oaks sways with the breeze. Three large manatees barely move as they hang out under the shade of the trees near the bank. Another large one swims slowly across the water, its tail flapping up and down, doing its lawn mower thing.

"Ms. Manatee," Deion says in his fake deep reporter voice,

"tell us how it feels to be the world's foremost authority on viral dolphin-manatee videos."

I snicker and turn serious. "I'd rather be a manatee expert than a viral video one."

"Yeah, but everyone pays attention to you now," Amelia says. "Look how quickly everyone agreed to try to get the dolphin back to the Gulf once you said to do it on the video."

I blush. It was strange when I put up a video interviewing the FWC scientist about the dolphin and how it should be returned to the Gulf, and immediately after, the FWC was inundated with emails and petitions to save the dolphin. "I think they were going to save the dolphin anyway and didn't need my help."

"They didn't need it, but they got it," Deion says.

I'm slowly getting used to the idea of being an internet personality. Dad is on board, helping me with my "branding" and coming up with ideas to spread my show. He's spearheading the new manatee festival our town's going to put on, and I'll even have a booth where I'll livestream Ms. Manatee.

As for our science project, Ms. Amato told us if we could put together a PSA that includes information about our whole experience with the viral video and the city council, that would count as our science project. We'll even get extra credit in social studies. Deion, Amelia, and I will turn right to it, after this visit to the springs.

But coming into the refuge, we saw the same girl in the parking lot, still fighting the new connector toll roads that will open up this area to development and more boats, visitors, and people. I'm glad we are making a difference in our town with the PSA and the new festival, but there's still a lot of work to do.

I scan the waters. The only thing that would make this the most perfect day ever is—

I see them. Coming into the cove are Missy, with her Y-shaped scar, and Sunny trailing close behind! I grip Deion's and Amelia's arms. "It's Missy and Sunny!" It's been so long since I've seen them.

"Hello, there, Missy and Sunny," Amelia says.

"Missy and Sunny, the two coolest manatees on the planet," Deion says.

I lean back, taking in the wonderful sight of my two best friends on land heaping love on my two best friends in the water.

Author's Note

The events, characters, and locations in this story are fictitious, but the dangers manatees face are real. In 2019, a record number of manatees were killed by boat strikes in Florida—136 manatees. Another 470 manatee deaths were recorded that year from natural causes, cold stress, and other reasons. In addition to boat strikes, manatees get tangled in fishing gear, fall ill from red tide algae blooms (exacerbated by warming waters, pollution, and runoff), become cold-stunned, and lose their habitats. All these dangers increase with growing numbers of people moving into areas where manatees live and roam.

While a friendship between a dolphin and a manatee like the one in this story would be very unusual, scientists have found these curious creatures do sometimes hang around each other. As noted in the story, saltwater dolphins can't stay too long in fresh water because they get exhausted from being less buoyant and their skin can slough off without the protective salt water.

To learn more about manatees, visit the Florida Fish and Wildlife Conservation Commission's website (myfwc.com/wildlifehabitats/wildlife/manatee), or the nonprofit group Save the Manatee Club (savethemanatee.org). In reality, a manatee festival does exist. For over thirty years, the town of Crystal River, Florida, has held an annual festival to celebrate manatees.

Acknowledgments

I am so thankful for the many people who helped create this book.

First, a huge thanks to my amazing agent, Jennifer March Soloway, for always believing in me. You knew this was the perfect story for me, and I couldn't imagine a better advocate and professional partner.

Thank you to my wonderful editor, Maya Marlette. Your kindness and brilliance shone through in every edit. I'm grateful to the Scholastic team, including Stephanie Yang, Caroline Flanagan, David Levithan, Mallory Kass, Elizabeth Parisi, Victoria Velez, Jessica White, Priscilla Eakeley, Jody Corbett, and Leni Villarreal.

I'm so grateful to my critique partners and early readers. Thanks to Elaine Kiely Kearns, Jessica Grace Kelley, Kimberly

Engebrigtsen, Megan E. McDonald, and Kim Tomsic for your insightful critiques; my Muse Writers workshop with Lydia Netzer, Mike Krentz, Jeanne Marie Liggio, John Cameron, Elaine Panneton, and Shannon Curtin; and early readers Hannah Capin, Teresa Robeson, Chris Braig, Bernadette Bartlett, and Katy Schuck.

Thank you, Kate Brauning, for your editorial advice and Breakthrough Writers' Boot Camp. Thanks to my mentors and teachers throughout my writing journey: Lydia Netzer, Ellen Bryson, and Michael Khandelwal at The Muse Writers Center and Tae Keller from Author Mentor Match.

I couldn't have written this book without expert advice. Thank you, Emily Davidson, former Batten Research Fellow and staff member of the Virginia Aquarium Stranding Response Program, for explaining manatee rescues and rehabilitation; Anne Harvey, staff attorney at Save the Manatee Club, for providing policy background; Ally Greco at Save the Manatee Club; Diane Ngai, formerly at Save the Manatee Club; Ennis Johnson, volunteer at Virginia Aquarium & Marine Science Center; and Brittany Kaitlyn Knowles, for sharing your 2015 Capstone research paper done at

Nova Southeastern University, "Social Interactions Between Bottlenose Dolphin (*Tursiops truncates*) and Antillean Manatee (*Trichechus manatus manatus*) in Belize." Any mistakes I made are my own.

I'm grateful for those who shared your knowledge during my research trip to Crystal River, Florida. Thank you, Matthew Clemons, board member of Save the Manatee Club and former kayak tour guide, and Sue Clemons, former kayak tour guide, for guiding me on a kayak trip on the Chassahowitzka River. Thanks to Crystal River Middle School, Tammy Rall, Eric Townsend, and Deborah and Randy Hodges for opening your classes and community to me. Thanks to the guides at River Ventures for the incredible experience of swimming with manatees.

Thank you to my friends who joined me on my trip, Samantha Wetzler; Anna Mahkorkina; and Anna's daughter, Lili Couture. I'm grateful to you and the rest of my book club—Janet, Katy, Heather, Andrea, Lilly, Mia, Sally, Kelly, and Kendall—for enriching my life, reading and otherwise.

Thank you, Dorothy Shiloff Hughes, for your viral video insights.

My thanks and love to the Penguin Posse, Victoria Warneck, Reneé LaTulippe, Yvonne Mes, Elaine Kiely Kearns, and Teresa Robeson, for your years of friendship and support.

A million thanks to my family, David, Sammi, and Sarah; my parents, Bernard and Terry Liu; my sister, Vivian; and my in-laws, Alan and Susan Jacobs, for your love and unconditional support over the years.

And finally, thank you, readers and animal lovers who will raise your voices to make the world a better place.

Author photograph © by K. Woodard Photography

Sylvia Liu is a children's author inspired by oceans, ghost crabs, and kraken. She grew up in Caracas, Venezuela, attended Yale College and Harvard Law School, and practiced environmental law for a decade at the U.S. Department of Justice and the nonprofit environmental group Oceana. Her picture book, *A Morning with Grandpa*, illustrated by Christina Forshay, was a New Voices Award winner. Sylvia lives in Virginia with her husband, two daughters, and cat.